Action Front

Boyd Cable
(Ernest Andrew Ewart)

Action Front

Boyd Cable (Ernest Andrew Ewart)

© 1st World Library – Literary Society, 2004
PO Box 2211
Fairfield, IA 52556
www.1stworldlibrary.org
First Edition

LCCN: 2005901138

Softcover ISBN: 1-4218-1116-2
Hardcover ISBN: 1-4218-1016-6
eBook ISBN: 1-4218-1216-9

Purchase *"Action Front"*
as a traditional bound book at:
www.1stWorldLibrary.org/purchase.asp?ISBN=1-4218-1116-2

1st World Library Literary Society is a nonprofit
organization dedicated to promoting literacy by:

- Creating a free internet library accessible from any
  computer worldwide.
- Hosting writing competitions and offering book
  publishing scholarships.

Readers interested in supporting literacy
through sponsorship, donations or
membership please contact:
literacy@1stworldlibrary.org
Check us out at: www.1stworldlibrary.ORG
and start downloading free ebooks today.

Action Front
contributed by Tim, Ed & Rodney
in support of
1st World Library Literary Society

TO

MR. J. A. SPENDER

To whose recognition and appreciation of my work, and to whose instant and eager hospitality in the "Westminster Gazette" so much of these war writings is due, this book is very gratefully dedicated by

THE AUTHOR

FOREWORD

I make no apology for having followed in this book the same plan as in my other one, "Between the Lines," of taking extracts from the official despatches as "texts" and endeavoring to show something of what these brief messages cover, because so many of my own friends, and so many more unknown friends amongst the reviewers, expressed themselves so pleased with the plan that I feel its repetition is justified.

There were some who complained that my last book was in parts too grim and too terrible, and no doubt the same complaint may lie against this one. To that I can only reply that I have found it impossible to write with any truth of the Front without the writing being grim, and in writing my other book I felt it would be no bad thing if Home realized the grimness a little better.

But now there are so many at Home whose nearest and dearest are in the trenches, and who require no telling of the horrors of the war, that I have tried here to show there is a lighter side to war, to let them know that we have our relaxations, and even find occasion for jests, in the course of our business.

I believe, or at least hope, that in showing both sides of the picture I am doing what the Front would wish me to do. And I don't ask for any greater satisfaction than that.

BOYD CABLE.
May 1916.

CONTENTS

IN ENEMY HANDS

The last conscious thought in the mind of Private Jock Macalister as he reached the German trench was to get down into it; his next conscious thought to get out of it. Up there on the level there were uncomfortably many bullets, and even as he leaped on the low parapet one of these struck the top of his forehead, ran deflecting over the crown of his head, and away. He dropped limp as a pole-axed bullock, slid and rolled helplessly down into the trench.

When he came to his senses he found himself huddled in a corner against the traverse, his head smarting and a bruised elbow aching abominably. He lifted his head and groaned, and as the mists cleared from his dazed eyes he found himself looking into a fat and very dirty face and the ring of a rifle muzzle about a foot from his head. The German said something which Macalister could not understand, but which he rightly interpreted as a command not to move. But he could hear no sound of Scottish voices or of the uproar of hand-to-hand fighting in the trench. When he saw the Germans duck down hastily and squeeze close up against the wall of the trench, while overhead a string of shells crashed angrily and the shrapnel beat down in gusts across the trench, he diagnosed correctly that the assault had failed, and that the British gunners were again searching the German trench with shrapnel. His German guard said something to the other men, and while one of them remained at the loophole and fired an occasional shot, the others drew close to their prisoner. The first thing they did was to search him, to turn each pocket outside-in, and when they had emptied these, carefully feel all over his body for any concealed article. Macalister bore it all with great philosophy, mildly satisfied that he had no money to lose and no personal property of any value.

Their search concluded, the Germans held a short consultation, then one of them slipped round the corner of the traverse, and, returning a moment later, pointed the direction to Macalister and signed to him to go.

The trench was boxed into small compartments by the traverses, and in the next section Macalister found three Germans waiting for him. One of them asked him something in German, and on Macalister shaking his head to show that he did not understand, he was signaled to approach, and a German ran deftly through his pockets, fingering his waist, and, searching for a money-belt, made a short exclamation of disgust, and signed to the prisoner to move on round the next traverse, at the same time shouting to the Germans there, and passing Macalister on at the bayonet point. This performance was repeated exactly in all its details through the next half-dozen traverses, the only exception being that in one an excitable German, making violent motions with a bayonet as he appeared round the corner, insisted on his holding his hands over his head.

At about the sixth traverse a German spoke to him in fairly good, although strongly accented, English. He asked Macalister his rank and regiment, and Macalister, knowing that the name on his shoulder-straps would expose any attempt at deceit, gave these. Another man asked something in German, which apparently he requested the English speaker to translate.

"He say," interpreted the other, "Why you English war have made?" Macalister stared at him. "I'm no English," he returned composedly. "I'm a Scot."

"That the worse is," said the interpreter angrily. "Why have it your business of the Scot?"

Macalister knitted his brows over this. "You mean, I suppose, what business is it of ours! Well, it's just Scotland's a bit of Britain, so when Britain's at war, we are at war."

A demand for an interpretation of this delayed the proceedings a little, and then the English speaker returned to the attack.

"For why haf Britain this war made!" he demanded.

"We didna' make it," returned Macalister. "Germany began it." Excited comment on the translation.

"If you'll just listen to me a minute," said Macalister deliberately, "I can prove I am right. Sir Edward Grey -" Bursts of exclamation greeted the name, and Macalister grinned slightly.

"You'll no be likin' him," he said. "An' I can weel understan' it."

The questioner went off on a different line. "Haf your soldiers know," he asked, "that the German fleet every day a town of England bombard?"

Macalister stared at him. "Havers!" he said abruptly.

The German went on to impart a great deal of astonishing information - of the German advance on Petrograd, the invasion of Egypt, the extermination of the Balkan Expedition, the complete blockade of England, the deci-mation of the British fleet by submarines.

After some vain attempts to argue the matter and disprove the statements, Macalister resigned himself to contemptuous silence, only rousing when the German spoke of England and English, to correct him to Britain and British.

When at last their interest flagged, the Germans ordered him to move on. Macalister asked where he was going and what was to be done with him, and received the scant comfort that he was being sent along to an officer who would send him back as a prisoner, if he did not have him killed - as German prisoners were killed by the English.

"British, you mean," Macalister corrected again. "And, besides that, it's a lie."

He was told to go on; but as he moved be saw a foot-long piece of barbed wire lying in the trench bottom. He asked gravely whether he would be allowed to take it, and, receiving a somewhat puzzled and grudging assent, picked it up, carefully rolled it in a small coil, and placed it in a side jacket pocket. He derived immense gratification and enjoyment at the ensuing searches he had to undergo, and the explosive German that followed the diving of a hand into the barbed-wire pocket.

He arrived at last at an officer and at a point where a communication trench entered the firing trench. The officer in very mangled English was attempting to extract some information, when he was interrupted by the arrival from the communication trench of a small party led by an officer, a person evidently of some importance, since the other officer sprang to attention, clicked his heels, saluted stiffly, and spoke in a tone of respectful humility. The new arrival was a young man in a surprisingly clean and beautifully fitting uniform, and wearing a helmet instead of the cloth cap commonly worn in the trenches. His face was not a particularly pleasant one, the eyes close set, hard, and cruel, the jaw thin and sharp, the mouth thin-lipped and   shrewish. He spoke to Macalister in the most perfect English.

"Well, swine-hound," he said, "have you any reason to give why I should not shoot you?" Macalister made no reply. He disliked exceedingly the look of the new-comer, and had no wish to give an excuse for the punishment he suspected would result from the officer's displeasure. But his silence did not save him.

"Sulky, eh, my swine-hound!" said the officer. "But I think we can improve those manners."

He gave an order in German, and a couple of men stepped forward and placed their bayonets with the points touching Macalister's chest.

"If you do not answer next time I speak," he said smoothly, "I will give one word that will pin you to the trench wall and leave you there. Do you understand!" he snapped suddenly and savagely. "You English dog."

"I understand," said Macalister. "But I'm no English. I'm a Scot"

The crashing of a shell and the whistling of the bullets overhead moved the officer, as it had the others, to a more sheltered place. He seated himself upon an ammunition-box, and pointed to the wall of the trench opposite him.

"You," he said to Macalister, "will stand there, where you can get the benefit of any bullets that come over. I suppose you would just as soon be killed by an English bullet as by a German one."

Macalister moved to the place indicated.

"I'm no anxious," he said calmly, "to be killed by either a *British* or a German bullet."

"Say 'sir' when you speak to me," roared the officer. "Say 'sir.'"

Macalister looked at him and said "Sir" - no more and no less.

"Have you no discipline in your English army?" he demanded, and Macalister's lips silently formed the words "British Army." "Are you not taught to say 'sir' to an officer?"

"Yes - sir; we say 'sir' to any officer and any gentleman."

"So," said the officer, an evil smile upon his thin lips. "You hint, I suppose, that I am not a gentleman? We shall see. But first, as you appear to be an insubordinate dog, we had better tie your hands up."

He gave an order, and after some little trouble to find a cord, Macalister's hands were lashed behind his back with the bandage from a field-dressing. The officer inspected the tying when it was completed, spoke angrily to the cringing men, and made them unfasten and re-tie the lashing as tightly as they could draw it.

"And now," said the officer, "we shall continue our little conversation; but first you shall beg my pardon for that hint about a gentleman. Do you hear me - beg," he snarled, as Macalister made no reply.

"If I've said anything you're no likin' and that I'm sorry for masel', I apologize," he said.

The officer glared at him with narrowed eyes. "That'll not do," he said coldly. "When I say 'beg' you'll beg, and you will go on your knees to beg. Do you hear? Kneel!"

Macalister stood rigid. At a word, two of the soldiers placed themselves in position again, with their bayonets at the prisoner's breast. The officer spoke to the men, and then to Macalister.

"Now," he said, "you will kneel, or they will thrust you through."

Macalister stood without a sign of movement; but behind his back his hands were straining furiously at the lashings upon his wrist. They stretched and gave ever so little, and he worked on at them with a desperate hope dawning in his heart.

"Still obstinate," sneered the officer. "Well, it is rather early to kill you yet, so we must find some other way."

BOYD CABLE

At a sentence from him one of the men threw his weight on the prisoner's shoulders, while the other struck him savagely across the tendons behind the knees. Whether he would or no, his knees had to give, and Macalister dropped to them. But he was not beaten yet. He simply allowed himself to collapse, and fell over on his side. The officer cursed angrily, commanding him to rise to his knees again; the men kicked him and pricked him with their bayonet points, hauled him at last to his knees, and held him there by main force.

"And now you will beg my pardon," the officer continued. Macalister said nothing, but continued to stretch at his bonds and twist gently with his hands and wrists.

The officer spent the next ten minutes trying to force his prisoner to beg his pardon. They were long and humiliating and painful minutes for Macalister, but he endured them doggedly and in silence. The officer's temper rose minute by minute. The forward wall of the firing trench was built up with wicker-work facings and the officer drew out a thick switch.

"You will speak," he said, "or I shall flay you in strips and then shoot you."

Macalister said nothing, and was slashed so heavily across the face that the stick broke in the striker's hands. The blood rose to his head, and deep in his heart he prayed, prayed only for ten seconds with his hands loose; but still he did not speak.

At the end of ten minutes the officer's patience was exhausted. Macalister was thrust back against the trench wall, and the officer drew out a pistol.

"In five minutes from now," he gritted, "I'm going to shoot you. I give you the five minutes that you may enjoy some pleasant thoughts in the interval."

Macalister made no answer, but worked industriously at the

lashings on his wrists. The bandage stretched and loosened, and at last, at long last, he succeeded in slipping one turn off his hand. He had no hope now for anything but death, and the only wish left to him in life was to get his hands free to wreak vengeance on the dapper little monster opposite him, to die with his hands free and fighting.

The minutes slipped one by one, and one by one the loosened turns of the bandage were uncoiled. The trenches at this point were apparently very close, for Macalister could hear the crack of the British rifles, the clack-clack-clack of a machine gun at close range, and the thought flitted through his mind that over there in his own trenches his own fellows would hear presently the crack of the officer's pistol with no understanding of what it meant. But with luck and his loosened hands he would give them a squeal or two to listen to as well.

Then the officer spoke. "One minute," he said, "and then I fire." He lifted his pistol and pointed it straight at Macalister's face. "I am not bandaging your eyes," went on the officer, "because I want you to look into this little round, round hole, and wait to see the fire spout out of it at you. Your minute is almost up ... you can watch my finger pressing on the trigger."

The last coil slipped off Macalister's wrist; he was free, but with a curse he knew it to be too late. A movement of his hands from behind his back would finish the pressure of that finger, and finish him. Desperately he sought for a fighting chance.

"I would like to ask," he muttered hoarsely, licking his dry lips, "will ye no kill me if I say what ye wanted?"

Keenly he watched that finger about the trigger, breathed silent relief as he saw it slacken, and watched the muzzle drop slowly from level of his eyes. But it was still held pointed at him, and that barely gave him the chance he longed for. Only let the muzzle leave him for an instant, and he would ask no more. The officer was a small and slightly made man, Macalister, tall

BOYD CABLE

and broadly built, big almost to hugeness and strong as a Highland bull.

"So," said the officer softly, "your Scottish courage flinches then, from dying?"

While he spoke, and in the interval before answering him, Macalister's mind was running feverishly over the quickest and surest plan of action. If he could get one hand on the officer's wrist, and the other on his pistol, he could finish the officer and perhaps get off another round or two before he was done himself. But the pistol hand might evade his grasp, and there would be brief time to struggle for it with those bayonets within arm's length. A straight blow from the shoulder would stun, but it might not kill. Plan after plan flashed through his mind, and was in turn set aside in search of a better. But he had to speak.

"It's no just that I'm afraid," he said very slowly. "But it was just somethin' I thought I might tell ye."

The pistol muzzle dropped another inch or two, with Macalister's eye watching its every quiver. His words brought to the officer's mind something that in his rage he had quite overlooked.

"If there is anything you can tell me," he said, "any useful information you can give of where your regiment's head-quarters are in the trenches, or where there are any batteries placed, I might still spare your life. But you must be quick," he added "for it sounds as if another attack is coming."

It was true that the fire of the British artillery had increased heavily during the last few minutes. It was booming and bellowing now in a deep, thunderous roar, the shells were streaming and rushing overhead, and shrapnel was crashing and hailing and pattering down along the parapet of the forward trench; the heavy boom of big shells bursting somewhere behind the forward line and the roaring explosion of trench mortar bombs about the forward trench set the ground quivering and shaking. A shell burst close overhead, and involuntarily Macalister glanced up, only to curse himself next moment for missing a chance that his captor offered by a similar momentary lifting of his eyes. Macalister set his eyes on the other, determined that no such chance should be missed again.

But now, above the thunder of the artillery and of the bursting shells, they could hear the sound of rising rifle-fire. The officer must have glimpsed the hope in Macalister's face, and, with an oath, he brought the pistol up level again.

"Do not cheat yourself," he said. "You cannot escape. If a charge comes I shall shoot you first."

With a sinking heart Macalister saw that his last slender hope was gone. He could only pray that for the moment no attack was to be launched; but then, just when it seemed that the tide of hope was at its lowest ebb, the fates flung him another chance - a chance that for the moment looked like no chance; looked, indeed, like a certainty of sudden death. A soft, whistling hiss sounded in the air above them, a note different from the shrill whine and buzz of bullets, the harsh rush and shriek of the shells. The next instant a dark object fell with a swoosh and thump in the bottom of the trench, rolled a little and lay still, spitting a jet of fizzing sparks and wreathing smoke.

When a live bomb falls in a narrow trench it is almost certain that everyone in that immediate section will at the worst die suddenly, at the best be badly wounded. Sometimes a bomb may be picked up and thrown clear before it can burst, but the man who picks it up is throwing away such chance as he has of being only wounded for the smaller chance of having time to pitch the bomb clear. The first instinct of every man is to remove himself from that particular traverse; the teaching of experience ought to make him throw himself flat on the ground, since by far the greater part of the force and fragments

BOYD CABLE

from the explosion clear the ground by a foot or two. Of the Germans in this particular section of trench some followed one plan, some the other. Of the two men guarding the prisoner the one who was near the corner of the traverse leapt round it, the other whirled himself round behind Macalister and crouched sheltering behind his body. Two men near the corner of the other traverse disappeared round it, two more flung themselves violently on their faces, and another leapt into the opening of the communication trench. The officer, without hesitation, dropped on his face, his head pressed close behind the sandbag on which he had been sitting.

The whole of these movements happened, of course, in the twinkling of an eye. Macalister's thoughts had been so full of his plans for the destruction of the officer that the advent of the bomb merely switched these plans in a new direction. His first realized thought was of the man crouching beside and clinging to him, the quick following instinct to free himself of this check to his movements. He was still on his knees, with the man on his left side; without attempting to rise he twisted round and backwards, and drove his fist full force in the other's face; the man's head crashed back against the trench wall, and his limp body collapsed and rolled sideways. His mind still running in the groove of his set purpose, before his captor's relaxed fingers had well loosed their grip, Macalister hurled himself across the trench and fastened his ferocious grip on the body of the officer. He rose to his feet, lifting the man with a jerking wrench, and swung him round. The swift idea had come to him that by hurling the officer's body on top of the bomb, and holding him there, he would at least make sure of his vengeance, might even escape himself the fragments and full force of the shock. Even in the midst of the swing he checked, glanced once at the spitting fuse, and with a stoop and a heave flung the officer out over the front parapet, leaped on the firing step, and hurled himself over after him.

It must be remembered that the burning fuse of a bomb gives no indication of the length that remains to burn before it explodes the charge. The fuse looks like a short length of thin black rope, its outer cover does not burn and the same stream of sparks and smoke pours from its end in the burning of the first inch and of the last. There was nothing, then, to show Macalister whether the explosion would come before his quick muscles could complete their movement, or whether long seconds would elapse before the bomb burst. It was an even chance either way, so he took the one that gave him most. Fortune favored him, and the roar of the explosion followed his flying heels over the parapet.

The officer, dazed, shaken, and not yet realizing what had happened, had gathered neither his wits nor his limbs to rise when Macalister leaped down almost on top of him. The officer's hand still clung to the pistol he had held, but Macalister's grasp swooped and clutched and wrenched the weapon away.

"Get up, my man," he said grimly. "Get up, or I'll blow a hole in ye as ye lie."

He added emphasis with the point of the pistol in the other's ribs, and the officer staggered to his feet.

"Now," said Macalister, "you'll quick mairch - that way." He waved the pistol towards the British trench.

The officer hesitated.

"It is no good," he said sullenly. "I should be killed a dozen times before I got across."

"That's as may be," said Macalister coolly.

"But if you don't go you'll get your first killing here, and say naething o' the rest o' the dizen."

A shell cracked overhead, and the shrapnel ripped down along the trench behind them with a storm of bullets thudding into the ground about their feet.

BOYD CABLE

"I will make you an offer," said the officer hurriedly. "You can go your way and leave me to go mine."

"You'll mak' an offer!" said Macalister contemptuously. "Here" - and he waved the pistol across the open again. "Get along there."

"I will give you -" the officer began, when Macalister broke in abruptly.

"This is no a debatin' society," he said. "But ye'll no walk ye maun just drive."

Without further words he thrust the pistol in his pocket, grabbed and took one handful of coat at the back of the officer's neck and another at the skirt, and commenced to thrust him before him across the open ground. But the officer refused to walk, and would have thrown himself down if Macalister's grasp had not prevented it.

"Ye would, would ye?" growled the Scot, and seized his captive by the shoulders and shook him till his teeth rattled. "Now," he said angrily, "ye'll come wi' me or -" he broke off to fling a gigantic arm about the officer's neck -"or I'll pull the heid aff ye."

So it was that the occupants of the British trench viewed presently the figure of a huge Highlander appearing through the drifting haze and smoke at a trot, a head clutched close to his side by a circling arm, a struggling German half-running, half-dragging behind his captor.

Arrived at the parapet, "Here," shouted Macalister. "Catch, some o' ye." He jerked his prisoner forward and thrust him over and into the trench, and leaped in after him.

It was purely on impulse that Private Macalister flung his prisoner out of the German trench, but it was a set and reasoned purpose that made him drag his struggling captive back over the open to the British trench. He knew that the British line would not shoot at an obvious kilted High-lander, and he supposed that the Germans would hesitate to fire on one dragging an equally obvious German officer behind him. Either his reasoning or his blind luck held true, and both he and his captive tumbled over into the British trench unhurt. An officer appeared, and Macalister explained briefly to him what had happened.

"You'd better take him back with you," said the officer when he had finished, and glanced at the German. "He's not likely to make trouble, I suppose, but there are plenty of spare rifles, and you had better take one. What's left of your battalion has withdrawn to the support trench."

"I am an officer," said the German suddenly to the British subaltern? "I surrender myself to you, and demand to be treated as an honorable prisoner of war. I do not wish to be left in this man's hands."

"Wish this and wish that," said Macalister, "and much good may your wishing do. Ye've heard what this officer said, so rise and mairch, unless ye wad raither I took ye further like I brocht ye here." And he moved as if to scoop the German's head under his arm again.

"I will not," said the German furiously, and turned again to the subaltern. "I tell you I surrender -"

"There's no need for you to surrender," said the subaltern quietly. "I might remind you that you are already a prisoner; and I am not here to look after prisoners."

The German yielded with a very bad grace, and moved ahead of Macalister and his threatening bayonet, along the line and down the communication trench to the support trench. Here the Scot found his fellows, and introduced his prisoner, made his report to an officer, and asked and received permission to remain on guard over his captive. Then he returned to the corner of the trench where the remains of his own company were. He told them how he had fallen into the German trench and what had happened up to the moment the German officer came into the proceedings.

"This is the man," he said, nodding his head towards the officer, "and I wad just like to tell you carefully and exactly what happened between him an' me. Ye'll understaun' better if a' show ye as weel as tell ye. Weel, now, he made twa men tie ma' hands behind ma' back first - if ony o' ye will lend me a first field dressing I'll show ye how they did it."

A field dressing was promptly forthcoming, and Macalister bound the German's hands behind his back, overcoming a slight attempt at resistance by a warning word and an accompanying sharp twist on his arms.

"It's maybe no just as tight as mine was," said Macalister when he had finished, and stood the prisoner back against the wall. "But it'll dae. Then he made twa men stand wi' fixed bayonets against ma' breast, and when I hinted what was true, that he was no gentleman, he said I was to kneel and beg his pardon. And now you," he said, nodding to the prisoner, "will go down on your marrow-bones and beg mine."

"That is sufficient of this fooling," said the officer, with an attempt at bravado. "It's your turn, I'll admit; but I will pay you well -"

Macalister interrupted him-"Ye'll maybe think it's a bit mair than fooling ere I'm done wi' ye," he said. "But speakin' o' pay... and thank ye for reminding me. Ower there they riped ma pooches, an' took a'thing I had."

He stepped over to the prisoner, went expeditiously through his pockets, removed the contents, and transferred them to his own.

"I'm no saying but what I've got mair than I lost," he admitted to the others, who stood round gravely watching and thoroughly enjoying the proceedings. "But then they took all I had, an' I'm only taking all he has."

He pulled a couple of sandbags off the parapet and seated himself on them.

"To go on wi' this begging pardon business," he said, "If a couple o' ye will just stand ower him wi' your fixed bayonets.... Thank ye. I wouldna' kneel," he continued, "so one o' them put his weight on my shoulders -" He looked at one of the guards, who, entering promptly into the spirit of the play, put his massive weight on the German's shoulders, and looked to Macalister for further instructions.

"Then," said Macalister, "the ither guard gave me a swipe across the back o' the knees."

The "swipe" followed quickly and neatly, and the German went down with a jerk.

"That's it exactly," said Macalister, with a pleasantly reminiscent smile. The German's temper broke, and he spat forth a torrent of abuse in mixed English and German.

Macalister listened a moment. "I said nothing; so I think he shouldna' be allowed to say anything," he remarked judicially. His comment met with emphatic approval from his listeners.

"I think I could gag him," said one of his guards; "or if ye preferred it I could just throttle his windpipe a wee bit, just enough to stop his tongue and no to hurt him much."

With an effort the German regained his control. "There is no need," he said sullenly; "I shall be silent."

"Weel," resumed Macalister, "there was a bit o' chaff back and forrit between us, and next thing he did was to slap me across the face wi' his hand. Do ye think," he appealed to his audience, "it would brak' his jaw if I gave him a bit lick across it?"

He advanced a huge hand for inspection, and listened to the free advice given to try it, and the earnest assurances that it did not matter much if the jaw did break.

"Ye'll feenish him off presently onyway, I suppose?" said one, and winked at Macalister.

"Just bide a wee," answered Macalister, "I'm coming to that. I think maybe I'll no brak his jaw, for fair's fair, and I want to give as near as I can to what I got."

He leant forward and dealt a mild but tingling slap on the German's cheek.

"I think," he went on, "the next thing I got was a slash wi' a bit switch he pulled out from the trench wall. We've no sticks like it here, so I maun just do the best I can instead."

He leant forward and fastened a huge hand on the prisoner's coat-collar, jerked him to him, and, despite his frantic struggles and raging tongue, placed him face down across his knees and administered punishment.

"I think that's about enough," he said, and returned the choking and spluttering prisoner to his place between the guards.

"He kept me," he said, "on my knees, so I think he ought ... thank ye," as the German went down again none too gently. "After that he went on saying some things it would be waste o' time to repeat. Swine dog was about the prettiest name he had any use for. But there was another thing he did; ye'll see some muck on my face and on my jacket. It came there like this; he took hold o' me by the hair - this way." And Macalister proceeded to demonstrate as he explained.

"Then - my hands being tied behind my back you will remember, like this - it was easy enough for him to pull me over on my face - like this... and rub my face in the mud.... The bottom o' this trench is in no such a state a' filth as theirs, but it'll just have to do." He hoisted the German back to his knees. "Then I think it was after that the pistol and the killing bit came in." And Macalister put his hand to his pocket and drew out the officer's pistol which he had thrust there.

"He gave me five minutes, so I'll give him the same. Has ony o' ye a watch?"

A timekeeper stepped forward out of the little knot of spectators that crowded the trench, and Macalister requested him to notify them when only one minute of the five was left.

"My manny here was good enough," said Macalister, "to tell me he wouldna' bandage my eyes, because he wanted me to look down the muzzle of his pistol; so now," turning to the prisoner, "you can watch my finger pulling the trigger."

As the four minutes ebbed, the German's courage ran out with them. The jokes and laughter about him had ceased. Macalister's face was set and savage, and there was a cold, hard look in his eye, a stern ferocity on his mud and bloodstained face that convinced the German the end of the five minutes would also surely see his end.

"One minute to go," said the timekeeper. A sigh of indrawn breaths ran round the circle, and then tense silence. Outside the trench they were in the roar of the guns boomed unceasingly, the shells whooped and screwed overhead, and from oat in front came the crackle and roar of rifle-fire; and yet, despite the noise, the trench appeared still and silent. Macalister noted that, as he had noted it over there in the German trench.

"Time's up," said the man with the watch. The German, looking straight at the pistol muzzle and the cold eye behind

BOYD CABLE

the sights, gasped and closed his eyes. The silence held, and after a dragging minute the German opened his eyes, to find the pistol lowered but still pointing at him.

"To make it right and fair," said Macalister, "his hands should be loose, because I had managed to loose mine. Will one o' ye ... thank ye. It's no easy," continued Macalister, "to just fit the rest o' the program in, seeing that it was here a bomb fell in the trench, an' his men bein' weel occupied gettin' oot o' its way, I threw him ower the parapet and dragged him across to oor lines. Maybe ye'd like to try and throw me out the same way."

The German was perhaps a brave enough man, but the ordeal of those last five minutes especially had brought his nerve to near its breaking strain. His lips twitched and quivered, his jaw hung slack, and at Macalister's invitation he tittered hysterically. There was a stir and a movement at the back of the spectators that by now thronged the trench, and an officer pushed his way through.

"What's this?" he said. "Oh, yes! the prisoner. Well, you fellows might have more sense than heap yourselves up in a crowd like this. One solitary Krupp dropping in here, and we'd have a pretty-looking mess. Open out along the trench there, and keep low down. You can be ready to move in a few minutes now; we are being relieved here and are going further back. Now what about this prisoner? Who is looking after him?"

"I am, sir," said Macalister. "The Captain said I was to take him back."

"Right," said the subaltern. "You can take him with you when you go. They've got some more prisoners up the line, and you can join them."

It was here that the episode ended so far as Macalister was concerned, and his relations with the German officer thereafter were of the purely official nature of a prisoner's guard. There were some other indignities, but in these Macalister had no hand. They were probably due to the circulation of the tale Macalister had told and demonstrated, and were altogether above and beyond anything that usually happens to a German prisoner. They need not be detailed, but apparently the most serious of them was the removal of a portion of the black mud which masked the German's face, so as to leave a diamond-shaped patch, of staring cleanness over one eye, after the style of a music-hall star known to fame as the White-eyed Kaffir; the ripping of a small portion of that garment which permitted of the extraction of a dangling shirt into a ridiculous wagging tail about a foot and a half long, and a pressing invitation, accompanied by a hint from the bayonet point, to give an exposition of the goose-step at the head of the other prisoners whenever they and their escort were passing a sufficient number of troops to form a properly appreciative audience. Probably a Cockney-born Highlander was res-ponsible for these pleasantries, as he certainly was for the explanation he gave to curious inquirers.

"He's mad," he explained. "Mad as a coot; thinks he's the devil, and insists on wagging his little tail. I have to keep him marching with his hands up this way, because he might try to grab my rifle. Now, it's no use you gritting your teeth and mumbling German swear words, cherrybim. Keep your 'ands well up, and proceed with the goose-step."

But with all this Macalister had nothing to do. When he had returned as nearly as he could the exact sufferings he had endured, he was quite satisfied to let the matter drop. "I suppose," he said reflectively, when the officer had gone, after giving him orders to see the prisoner back, "as that finishes this play, we'll just need to treat ma lad here like an ordinary preesoner. Has ony o' ye got a wee bit biscuit an' bully beef an' a mouthful o' water t' gie the puir shiverin' crater!"

A BENEVOLENT NEUTRAL

"... *the enemy temporarily gained a footing in a portion of our trench, but in our counter-attack we retook this and a part of enemy trench beyond.*" - EXTRACT FROM OFFICIAL DESPATCH.

A wet night, a greasy road, and a side-slipping motor-bike provided the means of an introduction between Second Lieutenant Courtenay of the 1st Footsloggers and Sergeant Willard K. Rawbon of the Mechanical Transport branch of the A.S.C. The Mechanical Transport as a rule extend a bland contempt to motor-cycles running on the road, ignoring all their frantic toots of entreaty for room to pass, and leaving them to scrape as best they may along the narrow margin between a deep and muddy ditch and the undeviating wheels of a Juggernaut Mechanical Transport lorry. But a broken-down motor-cycle meets with a very different reception. It invariably excites some feeling compounded apparently of compassion and professional interest to the cycle, and an unlimited hospitality to the stranded cyclist.

This being well known to Second Lieutenant Courtenay, he, after collecting himself, his cycle, and his scattered wits from the ditch and conscientiously cursing the road, the dark, and the wet, duly turned to bless the luck that had brought about an accident right at the doorstep of a section of the Motor Transport. There were about ten massive lorries drawn up close to the side of the road under the poplars, and Courtenay made a direct line for one from which a chink of light showed under the tarpaulin and sounds of revelry issued from a melodeon and a rasping file. Courtenay pulled aside the flap, poked his head in and found himself blinking in the bright glare of an acetylene lamp suspended in the middle of a Mechanical Transport traveling workshop. The walls - tarpaulin over a wooden frame - were closely packed with an array of tools, and the floor was still more closely packed with a work-bench, vice and lathe, spare motor parts, boxes, and half a dozen men. The men were reading newspapers and magazines; one was manipulating the melodeon, and another at the vice was busy with the file. The various occupations ceased abruptly as Courtenay poked his head in and explained briefly who he was and what his troubles were.

"Thought you might be able to do something for me," he concluded, and before he had finished speaking the man at the vice had laid down his file and was reaching down a mackintosh from its hook. Courtenay noticed a sergeant's stripes on his sleeve, and a thick and most unsoldierly crop of hair on his head plastered back from the brow.

"Why sure," the sergeant said. "If she's anyways fixable, you reckon her as fixed. Whereabouts is she ditched?"

Ten minutes later Courtenay was listening disconsolately to the list of damages discovered by the glare of an electric torch and the sergeant's searching examination.

"It'll take 'most a couple of hours to make any sort of a job," said the sergeant. "That bust up fork alone - but we'll put her to rights for you. Let's yank 'er over to the shop."

Courtenay was a good deal put out by this announcement.

"I suppose there's no help for it," he said resignedly, "but it's dashed awkward. I'm due back at the billets now really, and another two or three hours late - whew!"

"Carryin' a message, I s'pose," said the sergeant, as together they seized the cycle and pushed it towards the repair lorry.

"No," said Courtenay, "I was over seeing another officer out this way." He had an idea from the sergeant's free and easy style of address that the mackintosh, without any visible badges and with a very visible spattering of mud, had concealed the fact that he was an officer, and when he reached the light he casually opened his coat to show his belts and tunic. But the sergeant made not the slightest difference in his manner.

"Guess you'd better pull that wet coat right off," he said casually, "and set down while I get busy. You boys, pike out, hit it for the downy, an' get any sleep you all can snatch. That break-down will be ambling along in about three hours an' shoutin' for quick repairs, so you'll have to hustle some. That three hours is about all the sleep comin' to you to-night; so, beat it."

The damaged cycle was lifted into the lorry and propped up on its stand and before the men had donned their mackintoshes and "beat it," the sergeant was busy dismembering the damaged fork. Courtenay pulled off his wet coat and settled himself comfortably on a box after offering his assistance and being assured it was not required. The sergeant conversed affably as he worked.

At first he addressed Courtenay as "mister," but suddenly - "Say," he remarked, "what ought I to be calling you? I never can remember just what those different stars-an'-stripes fixin's mean."

"My name is Courtenay and I'm second lieutenant," said the other. He was a good deal surprised, for naturally, a man does not usually reach the rank of sergeant without learning the meaning of the badges of rank on an officer's sleeve.

"My name's Rawbon - Willard K. Rawbon," said the sergeant easily. "So now we know where we are. Will you have a cigar, Loo-tenant?" he went on, slipping a case from his pocket and extending it. Courtenay noticed the solidly expensive get-up and the gold initials on the leather and was still more puzzled. He reassured himself by another look at the sergeant's stripes and the regulation soldier's khaki jacket. "No, thanks," he said politely, and struggling with an inclination to laugh, "I'll smoke a cigarette," and took one from his own case and lighted it. He was a good deal interested and probed gently.

"You're Canadian, I suppose?" he said. "But this isn't Canadian Transport, is it?"

"Not," said the sergeant "Neither it nor me. No Canuck in mine, Loo-tenant. I'm good United States."

"I see," said Courtenay. "Just joined up to get a finger in the fighting?"

"Yes an' no," said the sergeant, going on with his work in a manner that showed plainly he was a thoroughly competent workman. "It was a matter of business in the first place, a private business deal that -"

"I beg your pardon," said Courtenay hastily, reddening to his ear-tips. "Please don't think I meant to question you. I say, are you sure I can't help with that? It's too bad my sitting here watching you do all the work."

The sergeant straightened himself slowly from the bench and looked at Courtenay, a quizzical smile dawning on his thin lips. "Why now, Loo-tenant," he said, "there's no need to get het up none. I know you Britishers hate to be thought inquisitive - 'bad form,' ain't it! - but I didn't figure it that away, not any. I'd forgot for a minute the difference 'tween -" He broke off and looked down at his sleeve, nodding to the stripes and then to the lieutenant's star. "An' if you don't mind I'll keep on forgetting it meantime. 'Twon't hurt discipline, seeing nobody's here anyway. Y' see," he went on, stooping to his work again, "I'm not used to military manners an' customs. A year ago if you'd told me I'd be a soldier, *and* in the British Army, I'd ha' thought you clean loco."

Courtenay laughed. "There's a good many in the same British Army can say the same as you," he said.

"I was in London when the flare-up came, an' bein' interested in business I didn't ball up my intellect with politics an' newspaper war talk. So a cable I had from the firm hit me wallop, an' plumb dazed me. It said, 'Try secure war contract. One hundred full-powered available now. Two hundred delivery within month.' Then I began to sit up an' take notice. Y' see, I'm in with a big firm of auto builders - mebbe you know 'em - Rawbon an' Spedding, the Rawbon bein' my dad? No? Well, anyhow, I got the contract, got it so quick it made my head swim. Gee, that fellow in the War Office was buyin' up autos like I'd buy pipe-lights. The hundred lorries was shipped over, an' I saw 'em safe through the specified tests an' handed 'em over. Same with the next two hundred, an' this" - tapping his toe on the floor - "is one of 'em right here."

"I see how the lorry got here," said Courtenay, hugely interested, "but I don't see how you've managed to be aboard. You and a suit of khaki and a sergeant's stripes weren't all in the contract, I suppose?"

"Nope," said the sergeant, "not in the written one, mebbe. But I took a fancy to seein' how the engines made out under war conditions, an' figured I might get some useful notes on it for the firm, so I fixed it to come right along."

"But how?" asked Courtenay - "if that's not a secret."

"Why, that guy in the testin' sheds was plump tickled when I told him my notion. He fixed it all, and me suddenly discoverin' I was mistook for a Canadian I just said 'M-m-m' when anybody asked me. I had to enlist though, to put the deal through, an' after that there wasn't trouble enough to clog the works of a lady's watch. But there was trouble enough at the other end. My dad fair riz up an' screeched cablegrams at me when I hinted at goin' to the Front. He made out it was on the business side he was kickin', with the attitude of the

United States toward the squabble thrown in as extra. Neutrals, he said we was, benevolent neutrals, an' he wasn't goin' to have a son o' his steppin' outside the ring-fence o' the U-nited States Constitution, to say nothing of mebbe losin' good business we'd been doin' with the Hoggheimers, an' Schmidt Brothers, an' Fritz Schneckluk, an' a heap more buyers o' his that would rear up an' rip-snort an' refuse to do another cent's worth of dealing with a firm that was sellin' 'em autos wi' one hand an' shootin' holes in their brothers and cousins and Kaisers wi' the other. I soothed the old man down by pointing out I was to go working these lorries, and the British Army don't shoot Germans with motor-lorries; and I'd be able to keep him posted in any weak points, if, and as, and when they developed, so he could keep ahead o' the crowd in improvements and hooking in more fat contracts; and lastly, that the Schmidt customer crowd didn't need to know a thing about me being here unless he was dub enough to tell 'em. So I signed on to serve King George an' his missus an' kids for ever an' ever, or duration of war, Amen, with a mental footnote, which last was the only part I mentioned in mailing my dad, that I was a Benevolent Neutral. An' here I am."

"Good egg," laughed Courtenay. "Hope you're liking the job."

"Waal, I'll amit I'm some disappointed, Loo-tenant," drawled the sergeant. "Y' see I did expect I'd have a look in at some of the fightin'. I'm no ragin' blood-drinker an' bone-buster by profession, up-bringin', or liking. But it does seem sorter poor play that a man should be plumb center of the biggest war in history an' never see a single solitary corpse. An' that's me. I been trailin' around with this convoy for months, and never got near enough to a shell burst to tell it from a kid's firework. It ain't in the program of this trench warfare to have motor transport under fire, and the program is bein' strictly attended to. It's some sight too, they tell me, when a good mix-up is goin' on up front. I've got a camera here that I bought special, thinking it would be fun later to show round my album in the States an' point out this man being skewered on a bayonet an' that one being disrupted by a bomb an' the next lot charging a

BOYD CABLE

trench. But will you believe me, Loo-tenant, I haven't as much as set eye or foot on the trenches. I did once take a run up on the captain's 'Douglas,' thinking I'd just have a walk around an' see the sights and get some snaps. But I might as well have tried to break into Heaven an' steal the choir's harps. I was turned back about ten ways I tried, and wound up by being arrested as a spy an' darn near gettin' shot. I got mad at last and I told some fellows, stuck all over with red tabs and cap-bands and armlets, that they could keep their old trenches, and I didn't believe they were worth looking at anyway."

Courtenay was laughing again. "I fancy I see the faces of the staff," he choked.

"Oh, they ante-d up all right later on," admitted the sergeant, "when they'd discovered this column and roped in my captain to identify me. One old leather-face, 'specially - they told me after he was a General - was as nice as pie, an' had me in an' fed me a fresh meat and canned asparagus lunch and near chuckled himself into a choking fit when I told him about dad, an' my being booked up as a Benevolent Neutral. He was so mighty pleasant that I told him I'd like to have my dad make him a present of as dandy an auto as rolls in France. I would have, too, but he simply wouldn't listen to me; told me he'd send it back freight if I did; and I had to believe him, though, it seemed unnatural. But they wouldn't let me go look at their blame trenches. I tried to get this General joker to pass me in, but he wouldn't fall for it. 'No, no,' he gurgles and splutters. 'A Benevolent Neutral in the trenches! Never do, never do. We'll have to put some new initials on the Mechanical Transport,' he says, 'B.N.M.T. Benevolent Neutral! I must tell Dallas of the Transport that.' And he shooed me off with that."

The sergeant had worked busily as he talked, and now, as he commenced to replace the repaired fork, he was thoughtfully silent a moment.

"I suppose there's some dandy sna-aps up in those trenches,

Loo-tenant?" he said at last.

"Oh, well, I dunno," said Courtenay. "Sort of thing you see in the picture papers, of course."

"Them!" said the sergeant contemptuously. "I could make better sna-aps posin' some of the transport crowd in these emergency trenches dug twenty miles back from the front. I mean real pictures of the real thing - fellows knee-deep in mud, and a shell lobbing in, and such like - real dandy snaps. It makes my mouth water to think of 'em. But I suppose I'll go through this darn war and never see enough to let me hold up my head when I get back home and they ask me what was the war really like and to tell 'em about the trenches. I could have made out if I'd even seen those blame trenches and got some good snaps of 'em."

Courtenay was moved to a rash compassion and a still more rash promise.

"Look here, sergeant," he said, "I'm dashed if I don't have a try to get you a look at the trenches. We go in again in two days and it might be managed."

*   *   *   *   *

Three days later Sergeant Rawbon, mounted on the motor-cycle which he had repaired and which had been sent over to him, found all his obstacles to the trenches melt and vanish before a couple of passes with which he was provided - one readily granted by his captain on hearing the reason for its request, and one signed by Second Lieutenant Courtenay to pass the bearer, Sergeant Rawbon, on his way to the headquarters of the 1st Footsloggers with motor-cycle belonging to that battalion. The last quarter mile of the run to the headquarters introduced Sergeant Rawbon to the sensation of being under fire, and, as he afterwards informed Courtenay, he did not find the sensation in any way pleasant.

"Loo-tenant," he said gravely, "I've had some of this under fire performance already, and I tell you I finds it no ways nice. Coming along that last bit of road I heard something whistling every now an' then like the top note of a tin whistle, and something else goin' *whisk* like a cane switched past your ear, and another lot saying *smack* like a whip-lash snapping. I was riding slow and careful, because that road ain't exactly - well, it would take a lot of sandpapering to make it really smooth. But when I realized that those sounds spelt bullets with a capital B, I decided that road wasn't as bad as I'd thought, and that anything up to thirty knots wasn't outside its limits."

"Oh, you were all right," said Courtenay carelessly, "bullets can't touch you there, except a few long-distance ones that fall in enfilade over the village. From the front they go over your head, or hit that parapet along the side of the road."

"Which is comforting, so far," said the sergeant, "though, personally, I've just about as much objection to be hit by a bullet that comes over a village as any other kind."

They were outside the remains of a house in the cellar of which was headquarters, Courtenay having timed the sergeant to arrive at an hour when he, Courtenay, could arrange to be waiting at headquarters.

"Now we'll shove along down and round the trenches. I spoke to the O.C. and explained the situation - partly. He didn't raise any trouble so just follow me, and leave me to do any talking there is to do. You must keep your eyes open and ask any questions about things after. It would look a bit odd and raise remarks if the men saw me showing you round and doing the Cook's Tour guide business. And if you've brought that camera, keep it out of sight till I give you the word. When we get along to my own company's bit of trench I'll tell you, and you can take some snaps - when I'm not looking at you. Just tip the wink to any men about and they'll be quite pleased to pose or anything you like."

"Loo-tenant," said Sergeant Rawbon earnestly, "you're doin' this thing real handsome, and I won't forget it. If ever you hit the U-nited States -"

"Oh, that's all right," said Courtenay, "come along now."

"When we find your bunch," said Rawbon as they moved off, "if you could make some sort of excuse out loud, and fade from the scene a minute and leave me there with the men, I'll sure get some of the dandiest snaps I'd wish. I reckon it'll satisfy the crowd if I promise to send 'em copies. It will if they're anything like my lot in the Mechanical Transport."

They slid down into a deep and narrow and very muddy ditch that ran twistingly through the wrecked village. Courtenay explained that usually they could walk this part above ground, sheltered from bullets by the broken-down houses and walls, but that a good few shells had been coming over all day, and that in the communication trench they were safe from all shells but those which burst directly over or in the part they were in.

"You want to run across this bit," he said presently. "A high explosive broke that in this morning, and it can't be repaired properly till dark. You go first and wait the other side for me. Now - jump lively!"

Rawbon took one quick jumping stride to the middle of the gap, and another and very much quicker one beyond it, as a bullet smacked venomously into the broken side of the trench. Another threw a spurt of mud at Courtenay's heels as he made the rush. "A sniper watches the gap and pots at anyone passing," he explained to Rawbon. "It's fairly safe, because at the range he's firing a bullet takes just a shade longer to reach here than you take to run across. But it doesn't do to walk."

"No," said Rawbon, "and going back somehow I don't think I will walk. I can see without any more explainin' that it's no spot for a pleasant, easy little saunter." He stopped suddenly as a succession of whooping rushes passed overhead. "Gee!

What's that?"

"Shells from our own guns," said Courtenay, and took the lead again. In his turn he stopped and crouched, calling to Rawbon to keek down. They heard a long screaming whistle rising to a tempestuous roar and breaking off in a crash which made the ground shake. Next moment a shower of mud and earth and stones fell rattling and thumping about and into the trench.

"Coal-box," said Courtenay hurriedly. "Come on. They're apt to drop some more about the same spot."

"I'm with you," said Rawbon. "The same spot is a good one to quit, I reckon."

They hurried, slipping and floundering, along the wet trench, and turned at last into another zig-zag one where a step ran along one side, and men muffled in wet coats stood behind a loopholed parapet. Along the trench was a series of tiny shelters scooped out of the bank, built up with sand-bags, covered ineffectually with wet, shiny, waterproof ground-sheets. In these, men were crouched over scantily filled braziers, or huddled, curled up like homeless dogs on a doorstep. At intervals along the parapet men watched through periscopes hoisted over the top edge, and every now and then one fired through a loophole. The trench bottom where they walked was anything from ankle-to knee-deep in evil-looking watery mud of the consistency of very thin porridge. The whole scene, the picture of wet misery, the dirt and squalor and discomfort made Rawbon shiver as much from disgust as from the raw cold that clung about the oozing clay walls and began to bite through to his soaking feet and legs. Courtenay stopped near a group of men, and telling the sergeant to wait there a moment, moved on and left him. A puff of cold wet wind blew over the parapet, and the sergeant wrinkled his nose disgustedly. "Some odorous," he commented to a mud-caked private hunkered down on his heels on the fire-step with his back against the trench wall. "Does, the Boche run a glue factory or a fertilizer works around here?"

"The last about fits it," said the private grimly. "They made an attack here about a week back, and there's a tidy few fertilizin' out there now - to say nothin' of some of ours we can't get in."

Rawbon squirmed uneasily to think he should, however unwittingly, have jested about their dead, but nobody there seemed in any way shocked or resentful. The sergeant suddenly remembered his camera, and had thrust his hand under his coat to his pocket when the warning screech of an approaching shell and the example of the other men in the traverse sent him crouching low in the trench bottom. The trench there was almost knee-deep in thin mud, but everyone apparently took that as a matter of course. The shell burst well behind them, but it was followed imme-diately by about a dozen rounds from a light gun. They came uncomfortably close, crashing overhead and just in front of the parapet. A splinter from one lifted a man's cap from his head and sent it flying. The splinter's whirr and the man's sharp exclamation brought all eyes in his direction. His look of comical surprise and the half-dazed fashion of his lifting a hand to fumble cautiously at his head raised some laughter and a good deal of chaff.

"Orright," he said angrily. "Orright, go on; laugh, dash yer. Fat lot t' laugh at, seein' a man's good cap pitched in the mud."

"No use you feelin' that 'ead o' yours," said his neighbor, grinning. "You can't even raise a sick 'eadache out o' that squeak. 'Arf an inch lower now an' you might 'ave 'ad a nice little trip 'ome in an 'orspital ship."

"You're wrong there, Jack," said another solemnly. "That splinter hit fair on top of his nut, an' glanced off. You don't think a pifflin' little Pip-Squeak shell could go through *his* head?" He stepped up on the firing-step as he spoke, and on the instant, with a rush and crash, another "Pip-Squeak" struck the parapet immediately in front of him, blowing the top edge off it, filling the air with a volcano of mud, dirt, smoke, and shrieking splinters, and, either from the shock of the explosion or in an attempt to escape it, throwing the man off his balance on the ledge of the firing-step to sprawl full length in the mud. In the swirl of noise and smoke and flying earth Rawbon just glimpsed the plunging fall of a man's body, and felt a curious sickly feeling at the pit of his stomach. He was relieved beyond words to see the figure rise to his knees and stagger to his feet, dripping mud and filth, and swearing at the pitch of his voice. He paid no attention to the stutter of laughter round him as he retrieved his mud-encrusted rifle, and looked about him for his cap. The laughter rose as he groped in the thin mud for it, still cursing wildly; and then the sergeant noticed that the man who had lost his cap a minute before had quietly snatched up the other one from the firing-step, clapped it on his own head and pretended to help the loser to search.

"It was blame funny, I suppose," Rawbon told the lieutenant a few minutes after, as they moved from the spot. "Him chasin' round in the mud cussin' all blue about his 'blarsted cap'; and t'other fellow wi' the cap on his head and pretending to hunt for it, and callin' the rest to come help. I dessay I'll laugh some myself, if I remember it when I'm safe back about ten mile from here. Just at the moment my funny bone hasn't got goin' right after me expectin' to see that feller blowed to ribbons an' remnants. But them others - say, I've seen men sittin' comfortable in an armchair seat at a roof-garden vaudeville that couldn't raise as hearty a laugh at the prize antics of the thousand dollar star comedian, as them fellers riz on that cap episode."

"Well, it was rather funny, you know," said Courtenay, grinning a little himself.

"Mebbe, mebbe," said Rawbon. "But me - well, if you'll excuse it, I'll keep that laugh in pickle till I feel more like usin' it."

"You wanted to come, you know," said Courtenay. "But I won't blame you if you say you've had enough and head for home. As I told you before, this 'joy-riding' game is rather silly. It's bad enough us taking risks we have to, but -"

"Yes, you spoke that piece, Loo-tenant," said Rawbon, "but I want to see all there is on show now I'm here. Only don't expect me to shriek with hilarious mirth every time a shell busts six inches off my nose."

They had halted for a moment, and now another crackling string of light shells burst along the trench.

"There's another bunch o' humor arriving," said Rawbon. "But I don't feel yet like encoring the turn any;"

They moved on to a steady accompaniment of shell bursts and Courtenay looked round uneasily.

"I don't half like this," he said. "They don't usually shell us so at this time of day. Hope there's no attack coming."

"I agree with all you say, Loo-tenant, and then some. Especially about not liking it."

"I'm beginning to think you'd be better off these premises," said Courtenay. "I ought to be with my company if any trouble is coming off. And it might lead to questions and unpleasantness if you were found here - especially if you're a casualty, or I am."

"Nuff sed, Loo-tenant," said Rawbon promptly. "I don't want that sort o' trouble for various reasons. I'd have an everlastin' job explaining to my dad what I was doin' in the front seats o' the firing line. It wouldn't just fit wi' my bein' a Benevolent Neutral, not anyhow."

"We're only about thirty or forty yards from the Germ trench in this bit," said Courtenay. "Here, carry my periscope, and when I'm talking to some of the men just take a look quietly."

But Rawbon was not able to see much when, a little later, he had a chance to use the periscope. For one thing the short winter day was fading and the light was already poor; for another any attempt to keep the periscope above the parapet for more than a few seconds brought a series of bullets hissing and zipping over, and periscope glasses in those days were too precious to risk for mere curiosity's sake.

"We'll just have a look at the Frying Pan," said Courtenay, "and then you'll have seen about the lot. We hold a bit of the trench running out beyond the Pan and the Germs are holding the same trench a little further along. We've both got the trench plugged up with sandbag barricades."

They floundered along the twisting trench till it turned sharply to the right and ran out into the shallow hollow of the Frying Pan. It was swimming in greasy mud, and across the far side from where they stood Rawbon could see a breastwork of sandbags.

"We call this entrance trench the Handle, and the trench that runs out from behind that barricade the Leak. There's always more or less bombing going on in the Leak, and I don't know if it's very wise of you to go up there. We call this the Frying Pan because - well, 'into the fire,' you know. Will you chance it?"

"Why, sure; if you don't mind, Loo-tenant," said Rawbon, "I might as well see -" He was interrupted by a sudden crash and roar, running bursts of flaring light, hoarse yells and shouts, and a few rifle shots from somewhere beyond the barricade across the Leak. The work of the next minute was too fast and furious for Rawbon to follow or under-stand. The uproar beyond the barricade swelled and clamored, and the earth shook to the roar of bursting bombs. In the Frying Pan there was a sudden vision of confused figures, dimly seen through the swirling smoke, swaying and struggling, threshing and splashing in the liquid mud. He was just conscious of Courtenay shouting something about "Get back," of his being thrust violently back into the wide trench, of two or three figures crowding in after him, cursing and staggering and shooting back into the Frying Pan, of Courtenay's voice shouting again to "Stand clear," of a knot of men scrambling and heaving at something, and then of a deafening "Rat-tat-tat-tat," and the streaming flashes of a machine-gun. It stopped firing after a minute, and Rawbon, flattened back against a corner of the trench wall, heard an explanation given by a gasping private to Courtenay and another mud-bedaubed officer who appeared mysteriously from somewhere.

"Flung a shower o' bombs an' rushed us, sir," said the private. "They was over a-top o' us 'fore you could say 'knife.' Only two or three o' us that wasn't downed and was able to get back out o' the Leak an' across the Pan to here."

"We stopped them with the maxim," said Courtenay, "but I suppose they'll rush again in a minute."

He and the other officer conferred hastily. Rawbon caught a few words about "counterattack" and "quicker the better" and "all the men I can find," and then the other officer moved hurriedly down the trench and men came jostling and crowding to the end of the Handle, just clear of the corner where it turned into the Pan. A few sandbags were pulled down off the parapet and heaped across the end of the trench, the machine-gun was run close up to them and a couple of men posted, one to watch with a periscope, and the other to keep Verey pistol lights flaring into the Frying Pan.

Two minutes later the other officer returned, spoke hastily to Courtenay, and then calling to the men to follow, jumped the low barricade and ran splashing out into the open hollow with the men streaming after him. A burst of rifle fire and the shattering crash of bombs met them, and continued fiercely for a few minutes after the last of the counter-attacking party had swarmed out. But the attack broke down, never reached the barricade beyond the Pan, was, in fact, cut down almost as fast as it emerged into the open. A handful of men came limping and floundering back, and Courtenay, waiting by the machine-gun in case of another German rush, caught sight of the face of the last man in.

"Rawbon!" he said sharply. "Good Lord, man! I'd for-gotten - What took you out there?"

"Say, Loo-tenant," said Rawbon, panting hard. "There's no crossin' that mud puddle Fry-Pan. They're holding the barricade 'cross there; got loopholes an' shootin' through 'em. Can't we climb out an' over the open an' on top of 'em?"

"No good," said Courtenay. "They're sweeping it with maxims. Listen!"

Up to then Rawbon had heeded nothing above the level of the trench and the hollow but now he could hear the steady roar of rifle and maxim fire, and the constant whistle of bullets streaming overhead.

"I must rally another crowd and try'n' rush it," said Courtenay. "Stand ready with that maxim there. I won't be long."

"I've got a box of bombs here, sir," said a man behind him.

Courtenay turned sharply. "Good," he said. "But no - it's too far to throw them."

"I think I could just about fetch it, sir," said the man.

"All right," said Courtenay. "Try it while I get some men together."

"Here y' are, chum," said the man, "you light 'em an' I'll chuck 'em. This way for the milky coco-nuts!"

Rawbon watched curiously. The bomb was round shaped and rather larger than a cricket ball. A black tube affair an inch or two long projected from it and emitted, when lit, a jet of hissing, spitting sparks. The bomb-thrower seized the missile quickly, stepped clear of the sheltering corner of the trench, threw the bomb, and jumped back under cover. A couple of bullets slapped into the wall of the trench, and next moment the bomb burst.

"Just short," said the thrower, who had peeped out at sound of the report. "Let's 'ave another go."

This time a shower of bullets greeted him as he stepped out, but he hurled his bomb and stepped back in safety. A third he threw, but this time a bullet caught him and he reeled back with blood staining the shoulder of his tunic.

"You'll 'ave to excuse me," he remarked gravely to the man with the match. "Can't stay now. I 'ave an urgent appointment in *Blighty*.[Footnote: England. A soldier's corruption of the Hindustani word "Belati."] But I'll drink your 'ealth when I gets to Lunnon."

Rawbon had watched the throwing impatiently. "Look here," he said suddenly. "Just lemme have a whale at this pitching. I'll show 'em some curves that'll dazzle 'em."

The wounded man peered at him and then at his cap badge. "Now 'oo the blank is this?" he demanded. "Blimey, Joe, if 'ere ain't a blooming Universal Plum-an'-Apple Provider. 'Ere, 'oo stole the strawberry jam?"

"You let me in on this ball game," said Rawbon. "Light 'em and pass 'em quick, and see me put the Indian sign on that bunch."

A minute later Courtenay came back and stared in amazement at the scene. Two men were lighting and passing up bombs to the sergeant, who, standing clear out in the opening, grabbed and hurled the balls with an extraordinary prancing and dancing and arm-swinging series of contortions, while the crowded trench laughed and applauded.

"Some pitchin', Loo-tenant," he panted beamingly, stepping back into shelter. "Hark at 'em. And every darn one right over the plate. Say, step out here an' watch this next lot."

"No time now," said Courtenay hurriedly.

"They're strengthening their defense every minute. Are you all ready there, lads?"

"I don't know who this man is, sir," said a sergeant quickly. "But he's doing great work. Every bomb has gone in behind the parado there. He might try a few more to shake them before we advance."

"Behind the parakeet," snorted Rawbon. "I should smile. You watch! I'll put some through the darn loopholes for you. Didn't know I was pitcher to the Purple Socks, the year we whipped the League, did you? Gimme thirty seconds, Loo-tenant, and I'll put thirty o' these balls right where they live."

As he spoke he picked up two of the bombs from a fresh box and held them to the lighter. As he plunged out a shower of bullets spattered the trench wall about him, but without heeding these he began to throw. As the roar of the bursting bombs began, the bullets slowed down and ceased. "Keep the lights blazing," Rawbon paused to shout to the man with the pistol flares. "You slide out for the home base, Loo-tenant, and I'll keep 'em too busy to shoot their nasty little guns." He commenced to hurl the bombs again. Courtenay stepped out and watched a moment. Bomb after bomb whizzed true and hard across the hollow, just skimmed the breastwork, struck on the trench wall that showed beyond and a foot above it, and fell behind the barricade. Billowing smoke-clouds and gusts of flame leaped and flashed above the parapet. Courtenay saw the chance and took it. He plunged out into the lake of mud and plowed through it towards the barricade, the men swarming behind him, and the sergeant's bombs hurtling with trailing streams of sparks over their heads.

"Come on, son," said the sergeant. "You carry that box and gimme the slow match. I pitch better with a little run."

Courtenay reached the barricade and led his men over and round it without a casualty. The space behind the barricade was deserted - deserted, that is, except by the dead, and by some unutterable things that would have been better dead.

The lost portion of trench was recaptured, and more, the defense, demoralized by that tornado of explosions, was pushed a good fifty yards further back before the counter-attack was stayed.

At daybreak next morning Courtenay and the sergeant stood together on the road leading to the communication trench. Both were crusted to the shoulders in thick mud; Rawbon's cap was gone, and his hair hung plastered in a wet mop over his ears and forehead, and Courtenay showed a red-stained bandage under his cap.

"Rawbon," he said, "I feel rotten over this business. Here you've done some real good work - I don't believe we'd ever have got across without your bombing - and you won't let me say a word about it. I'm dashed if I like it. Dash it, you ought to get a V.C., or a D.C.M. at least, for it."

"Now lookahere, Loo-tenant," said Rawbon soothingly. "There's no need for you to feel peaked - not any. It was darn good of you to let me in on these sacred no-admittance-'cept-on-business trenches, and I'm plumb glad I landed in the mix-up. It would probably raise trouble for you if your boss knew you'd slipped me in; and it sure would raise everlasting trouble for me at home if my name was flourishin' in the papers gettin' an A.B.C. or D.A.M.N. or whatever the fixin' is. And I'd sooner have this" - slapping the German helmet that dangled at his belt - "than your whole darn alphabet o' initials. Don't forget what I told you about the dad an' those Schwartzeheimer friends o' his, the cousins o' which same friends I've been blowin' off the earth with bomb base-balls. Let it go at that, and never forget it, friend - I'm a Benevolent Neutral."

"I won't forget it," said Courtenay, laughing and shaking hands. He watched the sergeant as he bestrode the motor-cycle, pushed off, and swung off warily down the wet road into the morning mist.

"What was it that despatch said a while back!" he mused. "Something about 'There are few who appreciate or even understand the value of the varied work of the Army Service Corps.' Well, this lot was a bit more varied than usual, and I fancy it might astonish even the fellow who wrote that line."

DRILL

"Yesterday one of the enemy's heavy guns was put out of action by our artillery." - EXTRACT FROM DESPATCH.

"Stand fast!" the instructor bellowed, and while the detachment stiffened to immobility he went on, without stopping to draw breath, bellowing other and less printable remarks. After he had finished these he ordered "Detachment rear!" and taking more time and adding even more point to his remarks, he repeated some of them and added others, addressing abruptly and virulently the "Number" whose bungling had aroused his wrath.

"You've learnt your gun drill," he said, "learned it like a sulphur-crested cockatoo learns to gabble 'Pretty Polly scratch a poll'; why in the name of Moses you can't make your hands do what your tongue says 'as me beat. You, Donovan, that's Number Three, let me hear you repeat the drill for Action Front."

Donovan, standing strictly to attention, and with his eyes fixed straight to his front, drew a deep breath and rattled off:

"At the order or signal from the battery leader or section commander, 'Halt action front!' One orders 'Halt action front!' - At the order from One, the detachment dismounts, Three unkeys, and with Two lifts the trail; when the trail is clear of the hook, Three orders 'Limber drive on.'"

The instructor interrupted explosively.

BOYD CABLE

"You see," he growled, "you know it. Three orders 'Limber drive on.' You're Three! but did you order limber drive on, or limber drive off, or drive anywhere at all? Did you expect drivers that would be sitting up there on their horses, with their backs turned to you, to have eyes in the backs of their heads to see when you had the trail lifted, or did you be expectin' them to thought-read that you wanted them to drive on!"

Three, goaded at last to a sufficiency of daring, ventured to mutter something about "was going to order it."

The instructor caught up the phrase and flayed him again with it. "'Was going to,'" he repeated, "'was going to order it.' Perhaps some day, when a bullet comes along and drills a hole in your thick head, you will want to tell it you 'was going to' get out of the way. You maybe expect the detachment to halt and stand easy, and light a cigarette, and have a chat while you wait to make up your mind what you're going to say, and when you're going to say it! And if ever you get past recruit drill in the barracks square, my lad, and smell powder burnt in action, you'll learn that there's no such thing as 'going to' in your gun drill. If you're slow at it, if you fumble your fingers, and tie knots in your tongue, and stop to think about your 'going to,' you'll find maybe that 'going to' has gone before you make up your mind, and the only thing 'going to' will be you and your detachment; and its Kingdom Come you'll be 'going to' at that. And now we'll try it again, and if I find any more 'going to' about it this time it's an hour's extra drill a day you'll be 'going to' for the next week."

He kept the detachment grilling and grinding for another hour before he let them go, and at the end of it he spent another five minutes pointing out the manifold faults and failings of each individual in the detachment, reminding them that they belonged to the Royal Regiment of Artillery that is "The right of the line, the terror of the world, and the pride of the British Army," and that any man who wasn't a shining credit to the Royal Regiment was no less than a black disgrace to it.

When the detachment dismissed, and for the most part gravitated to the canteen, they passed some remarks upon their instructor almost pungent enough to have been worthy of his utterance. "Him an' his everlastin' 'Cut the Time!'"

"I'm just about fed up with him," said Gunner Donovan bitterly, "and I'd like to know where's all the sense doing this drill against a stop-watch. You'd think from the way he talks that a man's life was hanging on the whiskers of a half-second. Blanky rot, I call it."

"I wouldn't mind so much," said another gunner, "if ever he thought to say we done it good, but not 'im. The better we does it and the faster, the better and the faster he wants it done. It's my belief that if he had a gun detachment picked from the angels above he'd tell 'em their buttons and their gold crowns was a disgrace to Heaven, that they was too slow to catch worms or catch a cold, and that they'd 'ave to cut the time it took 'em to fly into column o' route from the right down the Golden Stairs, or to bring their 'arps to the 'Alt action front."

These were the mildest of the remarks that passed between the smarting Numbers of the gun detachment, but they would have been astonished beyond words if they could have heard what their instructor Sergeant "Cut-the-Time" was saying at that moment to a fellow-sergeant in the sergeants' mess.

"They're good lads," he said, "and it's me, that in my time has seen the making and the breaking and the handling and the hammering of gun detachments enough to man every gun in the Army, that's saying it. I had them on the 'Halt action front' this morning, and I tell you they've come on amazing since I took 'em in hand. We cut three solid seconds this morning off the time we have been taking to get the gun into action, and a second a round off the firing of ten rounds. They'll make gunners yet if they keep at it."

"Three seconds is good enough," said the other mildly.

"It isn't good enough," returned the instructor, "if they can make it four, and four's not good enough if they can make it five. It's when they can't cut the time down by another split fraction of a second that I'll be calling them good enough. They won't be blessing me for it now, but come the day maybe they will."

*   *   *   *   *

The battery was moving slowly down a muddy road that ran along the edge of a thick wood. It had been marching most of the night, and, since the night had been wet and dark, the battery was splashed and muddy to the gun-muzzles and the tops of the drivers' caps. It was early morning, and very cold. Gunners and drivers were muffled in coats and woolen scarves, and sat half-asleep on their horses and wagons. A thick and chilly mist had delayed the coming of light, but now the mist had lifted suddenly, blown clear by a quickly risen chill wind. When the mist had been swept away sufficiently for something to be seen of the surrounding country, the Major, riding at the head of the battery, passed the word to halt and dismount, and proceeded to "find himself on the map." Glancing about him, he picked out a church steeple in the distance, a wayside shrine, and a cross-road near at hand, a curve of the wood beside the road, and by locating these on the squared map, which he took from its mud-splashed leather case, he was enabled to place his finger on the exact spot on the map where his battery stood at that moment. Satisfied on this, he was just about to give the order to mount when he heard the sound of breaking brushwood and saw an infantry officer emerge from the trees close at hand.

The officer was a young man, and was evidently on an errand of haste. He slithered down the steep bank at the edge of the wood, leaped the roadside ditch, asked a question of the nearest man, and, getting an answer from him, came at the double past the guns and teams towards the Major. He saluted hastily, said "Mornin', sir," and went on breathlessly: "My colonel sent me across to catch you. We are in a ditch along the edge of the far side of this wood, and could just see enough of you between the trees to make out your battery. From where we are we can see a German gun, one of their big brutes, with a team of about twenty horses pulling it, plain and fair out in the open. The Colonel thinks you could knock 'em to glory before they could reach cover."

"Where can I see them from!" said the Major quickly.

"I'll show you," said the subaltern, "if you'll leave your horse and come with me through this wood. It's only a narrow belt of trees here."

The Major turned to one of his subalterns who was with him at the head of the battery.

"Send back word to the captain to come up here and wait for me!" he said rapidly. "Tell him what you have just heard this officer say, and tell him to give the word, 'Prepare for action.' And now," he said, turning to the infantryman, "go ahead."

The two of them jumped the ditch, scrambled up the bank, and disappeared amongst the trees.

A message back to the captain who was at the rear of the battery brought him up at a canter. The subaltern explained briefly what he had heard, and the captain, after interrup-ting him to shout an order to "Prepare for action," heard the finish of the story, pulled out his map, and pointing out on it a road shown as running through the trees, sent the subaltern off to reconnoiter it.

The men were stripping off their coats, rolling them and strapping them to the saddles and the wagon seats; the Numbers One, the sergeants in charge of each gun, bustling their gunners, and seeing everything about the guns made ready: the gunners examining the mechanism and gears of the gun, opening and closing the hinged flaps of the wagons, and tearing the thin metal cover off the fuses.

BOYD CABLE

It was all done smartly and handily, and one after another the sergeants reported their subsections as ready. Imme-diately the captain gave the order to mount, drivers swung themselves to their saddles, and the gunners to their seats on the wagons, and all sat quietly waiting for whatever order might come next.

The lifting of the mist had shown a target to the gunners on both sides apparently, and the roar and boom of near and distant guns beat and throbbed quicker and at closer intervals.

In three minutes the Major came running back through the wood, and the captain moved to meet him.

"We've got a fair chance!" said the Major exultingly. "One of their big guns clear in the open, and moving at a crawl. I want you to take the battery along the road here, sharp to the right at the cross-road, and through the wood. The Inf. tell me there is just a passable road through. Take guns and firing battery wagons only; leave the others here. When you get through the wood, turn to the right again, and along its edge until you come to where I'll be waiting for you. I'll take the range-taker with me. The order will be 'open sights'; it's the only way - not time to hunt a covered position! Now, is all that clear?"

"Quite clear," said the captain tersely.

"Off you go, then," said the Major; "remember, it's quick work. Trumpeter, come with me, and the range-taker. Sergeant-major, leave the battery staff under cover with the first line."

He swung into the saddle, set his horse at the ditch, and with a leap and scramble was over and up the bank and crashing into the undergrowth, followed by his trumpeter and a man with the six-foot tube of a range-finder strapped to the saddle.

Before he was well off the road the captain shouted the order to walk march, and as the battery did so the subaltern who had been sent out to reconnoiter the road came back at a canter.

"We can just do it," he reported; "it's greasy going, and the road is narrow and rather twisty, but we can do it all right."

The captain sent back word to section commanders, and the other two subalterns spurred forward and joined him.

"We go through the wood," he explained, "and come into action on the other side. The order is 'open sights,' so I expect we'll be in an exposed position. You know what that means. There's a gun to knock out, and if we can do it and get back quick before they get our range we may get off light. If we can't --" and he broke off significantly. "Get back and tell your Numbers One, and be ready for quick moving."

Immediately they had fallen back the order was given to trot, and the battery commenced to bump and rumble rapidly over the rough road. As they neared the cross-roads they were halted a moment, and then the guns and their attendant ammunition wagons only went on, turned into the wood, and recommenced to trot.

They jolted and swayed and slid over the rough, wet road, the gunners clinging fiercely to the handrails, the drivers picking a way as best they could over bowlders and between ruts. They emerged on the far side of the wood, found themselves in an open field, turned sharply to the right, and kept on at a fast trot. A line of infantry were entrenched amongst the trees on the edge of the wood, but their shouted remarks were drowned in the clatter and rattle and jingle of wheels and harness. Out on their left the ground rose very gently, and far beyond a low crest could be seen clumps of trees, patches of fields, and a few scattered farm? houses. At several points on this distant slope the White smoke-clouds of bursting shells were puffing and breaking, but so far there was no sign to be seen of any man or of any gun. When they came to where the Major was waiting he rode out from the trees, blew sharply on a whistle, and made a rapid signal with hand and arm. The guns and wagons had been moving along the edge of the wood in single file, but now at the shouted order each team swung abruptly to its left and commenced to move in a long line out from the wood towards the low crest, the whole movement being performed neatly and cleanly and still at a trot. The Major rode to his place in the center of the line, and the battery, keeping its place close on his heels, steadily increased its pace almost to a canter. The Major's whistle screamed again, and at another signal and the shouted orders the battery dropped to a walk. Every man could see now over the crest and into the shallow valley that fell away from it and rose again in gentle folds and slopes. At first they could see nothing of the gun against which they had expected to be brought into action, but presently some one discovered a string of tiny black dots that told of the long team and heavy gun it drew. Another sharp whistle and the Major's signal brought the battery up with a jerk.

"Halt! action front!" The shouted order rang hoarsely along the line. For a moment there was wild commotion; a seething chaos, a swirl of bobbing heads and plunging horses. But in the apparent chaos there was nothing but the most smooth and ordered movement, the quick but most exact following of a routine drill so well ground in that its motions were almost mechanical. The gunners were off their seats before the wheels had stopped turning, the key snatched clear, and the trail of the gun lifted, the wheels seized, and the gun whirled round in a half-circle and dropped pointing to the enemy. The ammunition wagon pulled up into place beside the gun, the traces flung clear, and the teams hauled round and trotted off. As Gunner Donovan's trail was lifted clear his yell of "Limber, drive on," started the team forward with a jerk, and a moment later, as he and the Number Two slipped into their seats on the gun the Number Two grinned at him. "Sharp's the word," he said: "d'you mind the time -" He was interrupted roughly by the sergeant, who had just had the target pointed out to him, jerking up the trail to throw the gun roughly into line.

"Shut yer head, and get on to it, Donovan. You see that target there, don't you?"

"See it a fair treat!" said Donovan joyfully; "I'll bet I plunk a bull in the first three shots."

Back in the wood the infantry colonel, from a vantage-point half-way up a tall tree, watched the ensuing duel with the keenest excitement.

The battery's first two ranging shots dropped in a neat bracket, one over and one short; in the next two the bracket closed, the shorter shot being almost on top of the target. This evidently gave the range closely enough, and the whole battery burst into a roar of fire, the blazing flashes running up and down the line of guns like the reports of a gigantic Chinese cracker. Over the long team of the German gun a thick cloud of white smoke hung heavily, burst following upon burst and hail after hail of shrapnel sweeping the men and horses below. Then through the crashing reports of the guns and the whimpering rush of their shells' passage, there came a long whistling scream that rose and rose and broke off abruptly in a deep rolling cr-r-r-rump. A spout of brown earth and thick black smoke showed where the enemy shell had burst far out in front of the battery.

The infantry colonel watched anxiously. He knew that out there somewhere another heavy German gun had come into action; he knew that it was a good deal slower in its rate of fire, but that once it had secured its line and range it could practically obliterate the light field guns of the battery. The battery was fighting against time and the German gunners to complete their task before they could be silenced. The first team was crippled and destroyed, and another team, rushed out from the cover of the trees, was fallen upon by the shrapnel tornado, and likewise swept out of existence.

Then another shell from the German gun roared over, to burst this time well in the rear of the battery.

The colonel knew what this meant. The German gun had got its bracket. The battery had ceased to fire shrapnel, and was pouring high-explosive about the derelict gun. The white bursts of shrapnel had given place to a series of spouting volcanoes that leaped from the ground about the gun itself. Another German shell fell in front of the battery and a good 200 yards nearer to it. A movement below attracted the colonel's attention, and he saw the huddled teams straighten out and canter hard towards the guns. He turned his glasses on the German gun again, and could not restrain a cry of delight as he saw it collapsed and lying on its side, while high-explosive shells still pelted about it.

The teams came up at a gallop, swept round the guns, and halted. Instantly they were hooked in, the buried spades of the guns wrenched free, the wheels manned, the trails dropped clashing on the limber hooks. And as they dropped, another heavy shell soared over burst behind the battery, so close this time that the pieces shrieked and spun about the guns, wounding three horses and a couple of men. The Major, mounted and waiting, cast quick glances from gun to gun. The instant he saw they were ready he signaled an order, the drivers' spurs clapped home, and the whips rose and fell whistling and snapping. The battery jerked forward at a walk that broke immediately into a trot, and from that to a hard canter.

Even above the clatter and roll of the wheels and the hammering hoof-beats the whistle and rush of another heavy shell could be heard. Gunner Donovan, twisted sideways and clinging close to the jolting seat, heard the sound growing louder and louder, until it sounded so close that it seemed the shell was going to drop on top of them. But it fell behind them, and exactly on the position where the battery had stood. Donovan's eye caught the blinding flash of the burst, the springing of a thick cloud of black smoke. A second later something shrieked hurtling down and past his gun team, and struck with a vicious thump into the ground.

"That was near enough," shouted Mick, on the seat beside him. Donovan craned over as they passed, and saw, half-buried in the soft ground, the battered brass of one of their own shell cartridges. The heavy shell had landed fairly on top of the spot where their gun had stood, where the empty cartridge cases had been flung in a heap from the breech. If they had been ten or twenty seconds later in getting clear, if they had taken a few seconds longer over the coming into action or limbering up, a few seconds more to the firing of their rounds, the whole gun and detachment ...

Gunner Donovan leaned across to Mick and shouted loudly.

But his remark was so apparently irrelevant that Mick failed to understand. A sudden skidding swerve as the team wheeled nearly jerked him off his seat, the crackling bursts of half a dozen light shells over the plain behind him distracted his attention for a moment further. Then he leaned in towards Donovan, "What was that?" he yelled. "What didjer say?"

Donovan repeated his remark. "Gawd - bless - old 'Cut-the-Time.'"

The battery plunged in amongst the trees, and into safety.

A NIGHT PATROL

"During the night, only patrol and reconnoitering engagements of small consequence are reported." - EXTRACT FROM DESPATCH.

"Straff the Germans and all their works, particularly their mine works!" said Lieutenant Ainsley disgustedly.

"Seeing that's exactly what you're told off to do," said the other occupant of the dug-out, "why grouse about it?"

Lieutenant Ainsley laughed. "That's true enough," he admitted; "although I fancy going out on patrol in this weather and on this part of the line would be enough to make Mark Tapley himself grouse. However, it's all in the course of a lifetime, I suppose."

He completed the fastening of his mackintosh, felt that the revolver on his belt moved freely from its holster, and that the wire nippers were in place, pulled his soft cap well down on his head, grunted a "Good-night," and dropped on his hands and knees to crawl out of the dug-out.

He made his way along the forward firing trench to where his little patrol party awaited his coming, and having seen that they were properly equipped and fully laden with bombs, and securing a number of these for his own use, he issued careful instructions to the men to crawl over the parapet one at a time, being cautious to do so only in the intervals of darkness between the flaring lights.

He was a little ahead of the appointed time; and because the trench generally had been warned not to fire at anyone moving out in front at a certain hour, it was necessary to wait until then exactly. He told the men to wait, and spent the interval in smoking a cigarette. As he lit it the thought came to him that perhaps it was the last cigarette he would ever smoke. He tried to dismiss the thought, but it persisted uncomfortably. He argued with himself and told himself that he mustn't get jumpy, that the surest way to get shot was to be nervous about being shot, that the job was bad enough but was only made worse by worrying about it. As a relief and distraction to his own thoughts, he listened to catch the low remarks that were passing between the men of his party.

"When I get home after this job's done," one of them was saying, "I'm going to look for a billet as stoker in the gas works, or sign on in one o' them factories that roll red-hot steel plates and you 'ave to wear an asbestos sack to keep yourself from firing. After this I want something as hot and as dry as I can find it."

"I think," said another, "my job's going to be barman in a nice snug little public with a fire in the bar parlor and red blinds on the window."

"Why don't you pick a job that'll be easy to get?" said the third, with deep sarcasm - "say Prime Minister, or King of England. You've about as much chance of getting them as the other."

Lieutenant Ainsley grinned to himself in the darkness. At least, he thought, these men have no doubts about their coming back in safety from this patrol; but then of course it was easier for them because they did not know the full detail of the risk they ran. But it was no use thinking of that again, he told himself.

He took his place in readiness, waited until one flare had burned out and there was no immediate sign of another being thrown up, slipped over the parapet and dropped flat in the mud on the other side. One by one the men crawled over and dropped beside him, and then slowly and cautiously, with the officer leading, they began to wend their way out under their own entanglements.

There may be some who will wonder that an officer should feel such qualms as Ainsley had over the simple job of a night patrol over the open ground in front of the German trench; but, then, there are patrols and patrols, or as the inattentive recruit at the gunnery class said when he was asked to describe the varieties of shells he had been told of: "There are some sorts of one kind, and some of another."

There are plenty of parts on the Western Front where affairs at intervals settled down into such a peaceful state that there was nothing more than a fair sporting risk attaching to the performance of a patrol which leaves the shelter of our own lines at night to crawl out amongst the barbed wire entanglements in the darkness. There have been times when you might listen at night by the hour together and hardly hear a rifle-shot, and when the burst of artillery fire was a thing to be commented on. But at other times, and in some parts of the line especially, business was run on very different lines. Then every man in the forward firing-trench had a certain number of rounds to fire each night, even although he had no definite target to fire at. Magnesium flares and pistol lights were kept going almost without ceasing, while the artillery made a regular practice of loosing off a stated number of rounds per night. The Germans worked on fairly similar lines, and as a result it can easily be imagined that any patrol or reconnoitering work between the lines was apt to be exceedingly unhealthy. Actually there were parts on the line where no feet had pressed the ground of No Man's Land for weeks on end, unless in open attack or counter-attack, and of these feet there were a good many that never returned to the trench, and a good many others that did return only to walk straight to the nearest aid-post and hospital.

The neutral ground at this period of Ainsley's patrol was a sea of mud, broken by heaped earth and yawning shell-craters; strung about with barbed wire entanglements, littered with equipments and with packs which had been cut from or slipped from the shoulders of the wounded; dotted more or less thickly with the bodies of British or German who had fallen there and could not be reached alive by any stretcher-bearer parties. Unpleasant as was the coming in contact with these bodies, Ainsley knew that their being there was of considerable service to him. He and his men crawled in a scattered line, and whenever the upward trail of sparks showed that a flare was about to burst into light, the whole party dropped and lay still until the light had burned itself out. Any Germans looking out could only see their huddled forms lying as still as the thickly scattered dead; could not know but what the party was of their number.

It was necessary to move with the most extreme caution, because the slightest motion might eaten the attention of a look-out, and would certainly draw the fire of a score of rifles and probably of a machine-gun. The first part of the journey was the worst, because they had to cover a perfectly open piece of ground on their way to the slight depression which Ainsley knew ran curling across the neutral ground. Wide and shallow at the end nearest the British trench, this depression narrowed and deepened as it ran slantingly towards the German; halfway across, it turned abruptly and continued towards the German side on another slant, and at a point about halfway between the elbow and the German trench, came very close to an exploded mine-crater, which was the objective of this night's patrol.

It was supposed, or at least suspected, that the mine-crater was being made the starting-point of a tunnel to run under the British trench, and Ainsley had been told off to find out if possible whether this suspicion was correct, and if so to do what damage he could to the mine entrance and the miners by bombing.

When his party reached the shallow depression, they moved cautiously along it, and to Ainsley's relief reached the elbow in safety. Here they were a good deal more protected from the German fire than they could be at any point, because from here the depression was fully a couple of feet deep and had its highest bank next the German trench. Ainsley led his men at a fairly rapid crawl along the ditch, until he had passed the point nearest to the mine-crater. Here he halted his men, and with infinite caution crawled out to reco-nnoiter. The men, who had been carefully instructed in the part they were to play, waited huddling in silence under the bank for his return, or for the fusillade of fire that would tell he was discovered. Immediately in front of the crater was a patch of open ground without a single body lying in it; and Ainsley knew that if he were seen lying there where no body had been a minute before, the German who saw him would unhesitatingly place a bullet in him. A bank of earth several feet high had been thrown up by the mine explosion in a ring round the crater, and although this covered him from the observation of the trench imme-diately behind the mine, he knew that he could be seen from very little distance out on the flank, and decided to abandon his crawling progress for once and risk a quick dash across the open. For long he waited what seemed a favorable moment, watched carefully in an endeavor to locate the nearer positions in the German trench from which lights were being thrown up, and to time the periods between them.

At last three lights were thrown and burned almost simultaneously within the area over which he calculated the illumination would expose him. The instant the last flicker of the third light died out, he leaped to his feet, and made a rush. The lights had shown him a scanty few rows of barbed wire between him and the crater; he had reckoned roughly the number of steps to it and counted as he ran, then more cautiously pushed on, feeling for the wire, found it, threw himself down, and began to wriggle desperately underneath. When he thought he was through the last, he rose; but he had miscalculated, and the first step brought his thighs in scratching contact with another wire. His heart was in his mouth, for some seconds had passed since the last light had died and he knew that another one must flare up at any instant. Sweeping his arm downward and forward, he could feel no wire higher than the one-which had pricked his legs. There was no time now to fiddle about avoiding tears and scratches. He swung over the wire, first one leg, then another, felt his mackintosh catch, dragged it free with a screech of ripping cloth that brought his heart to his mouth, turned and rushed again for the crater. As he ran, first one light, then another, soared upwards and broke out into balls of vivid white light that showed the crater within a dozen steps. It was no time for caution, and everything depended on the blind luck of whether a German lookout had his eyes on that spot at that moment. Without hesitation, he continued his rush to the foot of the mound on the crater's edge, hurled himself down on it and lay panting and straining his ears for the sounds of shots and whistling bullets that would tell him he was discovered. But the lights flared and burned out, leaped afresh and died out again, and there was no sign that he had been seen. For the moment he felt reasonably secure. The earth on the crater's rim was broken and irregular, the surface an eye-deceiving patchwork of broken light and black heavy shadow under the glare of the flying lights. The mackintosh he wore was caked and plastered with mud, and blended well with the background on which he lay. He took care to keep his arms in, to sink his head well into his rounded shoulders, to curl his feet and legs up under the skirt of his mackintosh, knowing well from his own experience that where the outline of a body is vague and easily escapes notice, a head or an arm, or especially and particularly a booted foot and leg, will stand out glaringly distinct. As he lay, he placed his ear to the muddy ground, but could hear no sound of mining operations beneath him. Foot by foot he hitched himself upward to the rim of the crater's edge, and again lay and listened for thrilling long-drawn minute after minute.

Suddenly his heart jumped and his flesh went cold. Unmistakingly he heard the scuffle and swish of footsteps on the wet ground, the murmur of voices apparently within a yard

BOYD CABLE

or two of his head. There were men in the mine-crater, and, from the sound of their movements, they were creeping out on a patrol similar to his own, perhaps, and, as near as he could judge, on a line that would bring them directly on top of him. The scuffing passed slowly in front of him and for a few yards along the inside of the crater. The sound of the murmuring voices passed suddenly from confused dullness to a sharp clearer-edged speech, telling Ainsley, as plainly as if he could see, that the speaker had risen from behind the sound-deadening ridge of earth and was looking clear over its top, Ainsley lay as still as one of the clods of earth about him, lay scarcely daring to breathe, and with his skin pringling. There was a pause that may have been seconds, but that felt like hours. He did not dare move his head to look; he could only wait in an agony of apprehension with his flesh shrinking from the blow of a bullet that he knew would be the first announcement of his discovery. But the stillness was un-broken, and presently, to his infinite relief, he heard again the guttural voices and the sliding footsteps pass back across his front, and gradually diminish. But he would not let his impatience risk the success of his enterprise; he lay without moving a muscle for many long and nervous minutes. At last he began to hitch himself slowly, an inch at a time, along the edge of the crater away from the point to which the German lookout had moved. He halted and lay still again when his ear caught a fresh murmur of guttural voices, the trampling of many footsteps, and once or twice the low but clear clink of an iron tool in the crater beneath him.

It seemed fairly certain that the Germans were occupying the crater, were either making it the starting-point of a mine tunnel, or were fortifying it as a defensive point. But it was not enough to surmise these things; he must make sure, and, if possible, bomb the working party or the entrance to the mine tunnel. He continued to work his way along the rim of the crater's edge. Arrived at a position where he expected to be able to see the likeliest point of the crater for a mine working to commence, he took the final and greatest chance. Moving only in the intervals of darkness between the lights, he dragged the mackintosh up on his shoulders until the edge of its deep collar came above the top of his head, opened the throat and spread it wide to disguise any outline of his head and neck, found a suitable hollow on the edge of the ridge, and boldly thrust his head over to look downwards into the hole.

When the next light flared, he found that he could see the opposite wall and perhaps a third of the bottom of the hole, with the head and shoulders of two or three men moving about it. When the light died, he hitched forward and again lay still. This time the light showed him what he had come to seek: the black opening of a tunnel mouth in the wall of the crater nearest the British line, a dozen men busily engaged dragging sacks-full of earth from the opening, and emptying them outside the shaft. He waited while several lights burned, marking as carefully as possible the outline of the ridge immediately above the mine shaft, endeavoring to pick a mark that would locate its position from above it. It had begun to rain in a thin drizzling mist, and although this obscured the outline of the crater to some extent, its edge stood out well against the glow of such lights as were thrown up from the British side.

It was now well after midnight, and the firing on both sides had slackened considerably, although there was still an irregular rattle of rifle fire, the distant boom of a gun and the scream of its shell passing overhead. A good deal emboldened by his freedom from discovery and by the misty rain, Ainsley slid backwards, moved round the crater, crept back to the barbed wire and under it, ran across the opening on the other side and dropped into the hole where he had left his men. He found them waiting patiently, stretched full length in the wet discomfort of the soaking ground, but enduring it philosophically and concerned, apparently, only for his welfare.

His sergeant puffed a huge sigh of relief at his return. "I was just about beginning to think you had 'gone west,' sir," he said, "and wondering whether I oughtn't to come and 'ave a look for you."

BOYD CABLE

Ainsley explained what had happened and what he had seen. "I'm going back, and I want you all to come with me," he said. "I'm going to shove every bomb we've got down that mine shaft. If we meet with any luck, we should wreck it up pretty well."

"I suppose, sir," said the sergeant, "if we can plant a bomb or two in the right spot, it will bottle up any Germans working inside?"

"Sure to!" said Ainsley. "It will cave in the entrance completely; and then as soon as we get back, we'll give the gunners the tip, and leave them to keep on lobbing some shells in and breaking up any attempt to reopen the shaft and dig out the mining party."

"Billy!" said one of the men, in an audible aside, "don't you wish you was a merry little German down that blinkin' tunnel, to-night!"

"Imphim," answered Billy, "I don't think!"

Ainsley explained his plan of campaign, saw that everything was in readiness, and led his party out. The misty rain was still falling, and, counting on this to hide them sufficiently from observation if they lay still while any lights were burning, they crawled rapidly across the open, wriggled underneath the wires, cut one or two of them - especially any which were low enough to interfere with free move-ment under them - and crawled along to the crater.

Ainsley left the party sprawling flat at the foot of the rim, while he crept up to locate the position over the mine shaft. Each man had brought about a dozen small bombs and one large one packed with high explosive. Before leaving the ditch, on Ainsley's directions, each man tied his own lot in one bundle, bringing the ends of the fuses together and tying them securely with their ends as nearly as possible level, so that they could be lit at the same time. Each man had with him one of those tinder pipe-lighters which are ignited by the sparks of a little twirled wheel. When Ainsley had placed the men on the edge of the crater, he gave the word, and each man lit his tinder, holding it so as to be sheltered from sight from the German trench, behind the flap of his mackintosh. Then each took a separate piece of fuse about a foot long, and, at a whispered word from Ainsley, pressed the end into the glowing tinder. Almost at the same instant the four fuses began to burn, throwing out a fizzing jet of sparks. Each man knew that, shelter them as they would from observation, the sparks were almost certain to betray them; but although some rifles began at once to crack spasmodically and the bullets to whistle over-head, each man went on with the allotted program steadily, without haste and without fluster, devoting all their attention to the proper igniting of the bomb-fuses, and leaving what might follow to take care of itself. As his length of fuse caught, each man said "Ready" in a low tone; Ainsley immediately said "Light!" and each instantly directed the jet of sparks as from a tiny hose into the tied bundle of the bomb-fuses' ends. The instant each man saw his own bundle well ignited, he reported "Lit!" and thrust the fuse ends well into the soft mud. Being so waterproofed as to burn if necessary completely under water, this made no difference to the fuses, except that it smothered the sparks and showed only a curling smoke-wreath. But the first sparks had evidently been seen, for the bomb party heard shoutings and a rapidly increasing fire from the German lines. A light flamed upward near the mine-crater. Ainsley said, "Now! -, and take good aim." The men scrambled to their knees and, leaning well over until they could see the black entrance of the mine shaft, tossed their bundles of bombs as nearly as they could into and around it. In the pit below, Ainsley had a momentary glimpse of half a dozen faces, gleaming white in the strong light, upturned, and staring at him; from somewhere down there a pistol snapped twice, and the bullets hissed past over their heads. The party ducked back below the ridge of earth, and as a rattle of rifle fire commenced to break out along the whole length of the German line, they lit from their tinder the fuses of a couple of bombs specially reserved for the purpose, and tossed them as nearly as they

BOYD CABLE

could into the German trench, a score of paces away. Their fuses being cut much shorter than the others, the bombs exploded almost instantly, and Ainsley and his party leapt down to the level ground and raced across to the wire.

By now the whole line had caught the alarm; the rifle fire had swelled to a crackling roar, the bullets were whistling and storming across the open. In desperate haste they threw themselves down and wriggled under the wire, and as they did so they felt the earth beneath them jar and quiver, heard a double and triple roar from behind them, saw the wet ground in front of them and the wires overhead glow for an instant with rosy light as the fire of the explosion flamed upwards from the crater.

At the crashing blast of the discharge, the rifle fire was hushed for a moment; Ainsley saw the chance and shouted to his men, and, as they scrambled clear of the wire, they jumped to their feet, rushed back over the flat, and dropped panting in the shelter of the ditch. The rifle fire opened again more heavily than ever, and the bullets were hailing and splashing and thudding into the wet earth around them, but the bank protected them well, and they took the fullest advantage of its cover. Because the depression they were in shallowed and afforded less cover as it ran towards the British lines, it was safer for the party to stay where they were until the fire slackened enough to give them a fair sporting chance of crawling back in safety.

They lay there for fully two hours before Ainsley considered it safe enough to move. They were, of course, long since wet through, and by now were chilled and numbed to the bone. Two of the men had been wounded, but only very slightly in clean flesh wounds: one through the arm and one in the flesh over the upper ribs. Ainsley himself bandaged both men as well as he could in the darkness and the cramped position necessary to keep below the level of the flying ballets, and both men, when he had finished, assured him that they were quite comfortable and entirely free from pain. Ainsley doubted this, and because of it was the more impatient to get back to their own lines; but he restrained his impatience, lest it should result in any of his party suffering another and more serious wound. At last the rifle fire had died down to about the normal night rate, had indeed dropped at the finish so rapidly in the space of two or three minutes that Ainsley concluded fresh orders for the slower rate must have been passed along the German lines. He gave the word, and they began to creep slowly back, moving again only when no lights were burning.

There were some gaspings and groanings as the men commenced to move their stiffened limbs.

"I never knew," gasped one, "as I'd so many joints in my backbone, and that each one of them could hold so many aches."

"Same like!" said another. "If you'll listen, you can hear my knees and hips creaking like the rusty hinges of an old barn-door."

Although the men spoke in low tones, Ainsley whispered a stern command for silence.

"We're not so far away," he said, "but that a voice might carry; and you can bet they're jumpy enough for the rest of the night to shoot at the shadow of a whisper. Now come along, and keep low, and drop the instant a light flares."

They crawled back a score or so of yards that brought them to the elbow-turn of the depression. The bank of the turn was practically the last cover they could count upon, because here the ditch shallowed and widened and was, in addition, more or less open to enfilading fire from the German side.

Ainsley halted the men and whispered to them that as soon as they cleared the ditch they were to crawl out into open order, starting as soon as darkness fell after the next light. Next moment they commenced to move, and as they did so Ainsley fancied he heard a stealthy rustling in the grass immediately in front of him. It occurred to him that their long delay might have led to the sending out of a search party, and he was on the point of whispering an order back to the men to halt, while he investigated, when a couple of pistol lights flared upwards, lighting the ground immediately about them. To his surprise - surprise was his only feeling for the moment - he found himself staring into a bearded face not six feet from his own, and above the face was the little round flat cap that marked the man a German.

Both he and the German saw each other at the same instant; but because the same imminent peril was over each, each instinctively dropped flat to the wet ground. Ainsley had just time to glimpse the movement of other three or four gray-coated figures as they also fell flat. Next instant, he heard his sergeant's voice, hurried and sharp with warning, but still low toned.

"Look out, sir! There's a big Boche just in front of you."

Ainsley "sh-sh-shed" him to silence, and at the same time was a little amused and a great deal relieved to hear the German in front of him similarly hush down the few low exclamations of his party. The flare was still burning, and Ainsley, twisting his head, was able to look across the muddy grass at the German eyes staring anxiously into his own.

"Do not move!" said Ainsley, wondering to himself if the man understood English, and fumbling in vain in his mind for the German phrase that would express his meaning.

"Kamarade - eh?" grunted the German, with a note of interrogation that left no doubt as to his meaning.

"Nein, nein!" answered Ainsley. "You kamarade - sie kamarade."

The other, in somewhat voluble gutturals, insisted that Ainsley must "kamarade," otherwise surrender. He spoke too fast for Ainsley's very limited knowledge of German to follow, but at least, to Ainsley's relief, there was for the moment no motion towards hostilities on either side. The Germans recognized, no doubt as he did, that the first sign of a shot, the first wink of a rifle flash out there in the open, would bring upon them a blaze of light and a storm of rifle and maxim bullets. Even although his party had slightly the advantage of position in the scanty cover of the ditch, he was not at all inclined to bring about another burst of firing, particularly as he was not sure that some excitable individuals in his own trench would not forget about his party being in the open and hail indiscriminate bullets in the direction of a rifle flash, or even the sound of indiscreetly loud talking.

Painfully, in very broken German, and a word or two at a time, he tried to make his enemy understand that it was his, the German party, that must surrender, pointing out as an argument that they were nearer to the British than to the German lines. The German, however, discounted this argument by stating that he had one more man in his party than Ainsley had, and must therefore claim the privilege of being captor.

The voice of his own sergeant close behind him spoke in a hoarse undertone: "Shall I blow a blinkin' 'ole in 'im, sir? I could do 'im in acrost your shoulder, as easy as kiss my 'and."

"No, no!" said Ainsley hurriedly; "a shot here would raise the mischief."

At the same time he heard some of the other Germans speak to the man in front of him and discovered that they were addressing him as "Sergeant."

"Sie ein sergeant?" he questioned, and on the German admitting that he was a sergeant, Ainsley, with more fumbling after German words and phrases, explained that he was an officer, and that therefore his, an officer's patrol, took

BOYD CABLE

precedence over that of a mere sergeant. He had a good deal of difficulty in making this clear to the German - either because the sergeant was particularly thick-witted or possibly because Ainsley's German was particularly bad. Ainsley inclined to put it down to the German's stupidity, and he began to grow exceedingly wroth over the business. Naturally it never occurred to him that he should surrender to the German, but it annoyed him exceedingly that the German should have any similar feelings about surren-dering to him. Once more he bent his persuasive powers and indifferent German to the task of over-persuading the sergeant, and in return had to wait and slowly unravel some meaning from the odd words he could catch here and there in the sergeant's endeavor to over-persuade him.

He began to think at last that there was no way out of it but that suggested by his own sergeant - namely, to "blow a blinkin' 'ole in 'im," and his sergeant spoke again with the rattle of his chattering teeth playing a castanet accompa-niment to his words.

"If you don't mind, sir, we'd all like to fight it out and make a run for it. We're all about froze stiff."

"I'm just about fed up with this fool, too," said Ainsley disgustedly. "Look here, all of you! Watch me when the next light goes up. If you see me grab my pistol, pick your man and shoot."

The voice of the German sergeant broke in: -

"Nein, nein!" and then in English: "You no shoot! You shoot, and uns shoot alzo!"

Ainsley listened to the stammering English in an amaze-ment that gave way to overwhelming anger. "Here," he said angrily, "can you speak English?"

"Ein leetle, just ein leetle," replied the German.

But at that and at the memory of the long minutes spent there lying in the mud with chilled and frozen limbs trying to talk in German, at the time wasted, at his own stumbling German and the probable amusement his grammatical mistakes had given the others - the last, the Englishman's dislike to being laughed at, being perhaps the strongest factor - Ainsley's anger overcame him.

"You miserable blighter!" he said wrathfully. "You have the blazing cheek to keep me lying here in this filthy muck, mumbling and bungling over your beastly German, and then calmly tell me that you understand English all the time.

"Why couldn't you *say* you spoke English? What! D'you think I've nothing better to do than lie out here in a puddle of mud listening to you jabbering your beastly lingo? Silly ass! You saw that I didn't know German properly, to begin with - why couldn't you say you spoke English?"

But in his anger he had raised his voice a good deal above the safety limit, and the quick crackle of rifle fire and the soaring lights told that his voice had been heard, that the party or parties were discovered or suspected.

The rest followed so quickly, the action was so rapid and unpremeditated, that Ainsley never quite remembered its sequence. He has a confused memory of seeing the wet ground illumined by many lights, of drumming rifle fire and hissing bullets, and then, immediately after, the rush and crash of a couple of German "Fizz-Bang" shells. Probably it was the wet *plop* of some of the backward-flung bullets about him, possibly it was the movement of the German sergeant that wiped out the instinctive desire to flatten himself close to ground that drove him to instant action. The sergeant half lurched to his knees, thrusting forward the muzzle of his rifle. Ainsley clutched at the revolver in his holster, but before he could free it another shell crashed, the German jerked forward as if struck by a battering-ram between the shoulders, lay with white fingers clawing and clutching at the muddy grass. A momentary darkness fell, and Ainsley just had a glimpse of a knot of struggling figures, of the knot's falling apart with a clash of steel, of a rifle spouting a long tongue of flame ... and then a group of lights blazed again and disclosed the figures of his own three men crouching and glancing about them.

Of all these happenings Ainsley retains only a very jumbled recollection, but he remembers very distinctly his savage satisfaction at seeing "that fool sergeant" downed and the unappeased anger he still felt with him. He carried that anger back to his own trench; it still burned hot in him as they floundered and wallowed for interminable seconds over the greasy mud with the bullets slapping and smacking about them, as they wrenched and struggled over their own wire - where Ainsley, as it happened, had to wait to help his sergeant, who for all the advantage of their initiative in the attack and in the Germans being barely risen to meet it, had been caught by a bayonet-thrust in the thigh - the scramble across the parapet and hurried roll over into the waterlogged trench.

He arrived there wet to the skin and chilled to the bone, with his shoulder stinging abominably from the ragged tear of a ricochet bullet that had caught him in the last second on the parapet, and, above all, still filled with a consuming anger against the German sergeant. Five minutes later, in the Battalion H.Q. dugout, in making his report to the O.C. while the Medical dressed his arm, he only gave the barest and briefest account of his successful patrol and bombing work, but descanted at full length and with lurid wrath on the incident of the German patrol.

"When I think of that ignorant beast of a sergeant keeping me out there," he concluded disgustedly, "mumbling and spluttering over his confounded 'yaw, yaw' and 'nein, nein,' trying to scrape up odd German words - which I probably got all wrong - to make him understand, and him all the time quite well able to speak good enough English - that's what beats me - why couldn't he *say* he spoke English?"

"Well, anyhow," said the O.C. consolingly, "from what you tell me, he's dead now."

"I hope so," said Ainsley viciously, "and serve him jolly well right. But just think of the trouble it might have saved if he'd only said at first that he spoke English!" He sputtered wrathfully again: "Silly ass! Why couldn't he just *say* so?"

AS OTHERS SEE

"It may now be divulged that, some time ago, the British lines were extended for a considerable distance to the South." - EXTRACT FROM OFFICIAL DISPATCH.

The first notice that the men of the Tower Bridge Foot had that they were to move outside the territory they had learned so well in many weary marches and wanderings in networks and mazes of trenches, was when they crossed a road which had for long marked the boundary line between the grounds occupied by the British and French forces.

"Do you suppose the O.C. is drunk, or that the guide has lost his way?" said Private Robinson. "Somebody ought to tell him we're off our beat and that trespassers will be prosecuted. Not but what he don't know that, seeing he prosecuted me cruel six months ago for roving off into the French lines - said if I did it again I might be took for a spy and shot. Anyhow, I'd be took for being where I was out o' bounds and get a dose of Field Punishment. Wonder where we're bound for?"

"Don't see as it matters much," said his next file. "I suppose one wet field's as good as another to sleep in, so why worry?"

A little farther on, the battalion met a French Infantry Regiment on the march. The French regiment's road discipline was rather more lax than the British, and many tolerantly amused criticisms were passed on the loose formation, the lack of keeping step, and the straggling lines of the French. The criticisms, curiously enough, came in a great many cases from the very men in the Towers' ranks who had often "groused" most at the silliness of themselves being kept up to the mark in these matters. The marching Frenchmen were singing - but singing in a fashion quite novel to the British. Throughout their column there were anything up to a dozen songs in progress, some as choruses and some as solos, and the effect was certainly rather weird. The Tower Bridge officers, knowing their own men's fondness for swinging march songs, expected, and, to tell truth, half hoped that they would give a display of their harmonious powers. They did, but hardly in the expected fashion. One man demanded in a growling bass that the "Home Fires be kept Burning," while another bade farewell to Leicester Square in a high falsetto. The giggling Towers caught the idea instantly, and a confused medley of hymns, music-hall ditties, and patriotic songs in every key, from the deepest bellowing bass to the shrillest wailing treble, arose from the Towers' ranks, mixed with whistles and cat-calls and Corporal Flannigan's famous imitation of "Life on a Farm." The joke lasted the Towers for the rest of that march, and as sure as any Frenchman met or overtook them on the road he was treated to a vocal entertainment that must have left him forever convinced of the rumored potency of British rum.

By now word had passed round the Towers that they were to take over a portion of the trenches hitherto occupied by the French. Many were the doubts, and many were the arguments, as to whether this would or would not be to the personal advantage and comfort of themselves; but at least it made a change of scene and surroundings from those they had learned for months past, and since such a change is as the breath of life to the British soldier, they were on the whole highly pleased with it.

The morning was well advanced when they were met by guides and interpreters from the French regiment which they were relieving, and commenced to move into the new trenches. Although at first there were some who were inclined to criticize, and reluctant to believe that a French-man, or any other foreigner, could do or make anything better than an

Englishman, the Towers had to admit, even before they reached the forward firing trench, that the work of making communication trenches had been done in a manner beyond British praise. The trenches were narrow and very deep, neatly paved throughout their length with brick, spaced at regular intervals with sunk traps for draining off rain-water, and with bays and niches cut deep in the side to permit the passing of any one meeting a line of pack-burdened men in the shoulder-wide alley-way.

When they reached the forward firing trench, their admiration became unbounded; they were as full of eager curiosity as children on a school picnic. They fraternized instantly and warmly with the outgoing Frenchmen, and the Frenchmen for their part were equally eager to express friendship, to show the English the dugouts, the handy little contrivances for comfort and safety, to bequeath to their successors all sorts of stoves and pots and cooking utensils, and generally to give an impression, which was put into words by Private Robinson: "Strike me if this ain't the most cordiawl bloomin' ongtongt I've ever met!"

The Towers had never realized, or regretted, their lack of the French as deeply as they came to do now. Hitherto dealings in the language had been entirely with the women in the villages and billets of the reserve lines, where there was plenty of time to find means of expressing the two things that for the most part were all they had to express - their wants and their thanks. And because by now they had no slightest difficulty in making these billet inhabitants understand what they required - a fire for cooking, stretching space on a floor, the location of the nearest estaminets, whether eggs, butter, and bread were obtainable, and how much was the price - they had fondly imagined in their hearts, and boasted loudly in their home letters, that they were quite satisfactorily conversant with the French language. Now they were to discover that their knowledge was not quite so extensive as they had imagined, although it never occurred to them that the French women in the billets were learning English a great deal more rapidly and efficiently than they were learning French, that it was not altogether their mastery of the language which instantly produced soap and water, for instance, when they made motions of washing their hands and said slowly and loudly: "Soap - you compree, soap and l'eau; you savvy - l'eau, water." But now, when it came to the technicalities of their professional business, they found their command of the language completely inadequate. There were many of them who could ask, "What is the time?" but that helped them little to discover at what time the Germans made a practice of shelling the trenches; they could have asked with ease, "Have you any eggs?" but they could not twist this into a sentence to ask whether there were any egg-selling farms in the vicinity; could have asked "how much" was the bread, but not how many yards it was to the German trench.

A few Frenchmen, who spoke more or less English, found themselves in enormous French and English demand, while Private 'Enery Irving, who had hitherto borne some reputation as a French speaker - a reputation, it may be mentioned, largely due to his artful knack of helping out spoken words by imitation and explanatory acting - found his bubble reputation suddenly and disastrously pricked. He made some attempt to clutch at its remains by listening to the remarks addressed to him by a Frenchman, with a most potently intelligent and understanding expression, by ejaculating "Nong, nong!" and a profoundly understanding "Ah, wee!" at intervals in the one-sided conversation. He tried this method when called upon by a puzzled private to interpret the torrential speech of a Frenchman, who wished to know whether the Towers had any jam to spare, or whether they would exchange a rum ration for some French wine. 'Enery interjected a few "Ah, wee's!" and then at the finish explained to the private.

"He speaks a bit fast," he said, "but he's trying to tell me something about him coming from a place called Conserve, and that we can have his 'room' here - meaning, I suppose, his dug-out." He turned to the Frenchman, spread out his hands, shrugged his shoulders, and gesticulated after the most approved fashion of the stage Frenchman, bowed deeply, and said, *"Merci, Monsieur,"* many times. The Frenchman naturally looked a good deal puzzled, but bowed politely in reply and repeated his question at length. This producing no effect except further stage shrugs, he seized upon one of the interpreters who was passing and explained rapidly. "He asks," said the interpreter, turning to 'Enery and the other men, "whether you have any *conserve et rhum* - jam and rum - you wish to exchange for his wine." After that 'Enery Irving collapsed in the public estimation as a French speaker.

When the Towers were properly installed, and the French regiment commenced to move out, a Tower Bridge officer came along and told his men that they were to be careful to keep out of sight, as the orders were to deceive the Germans opposite and to keep them ignorant as long as possible of the British-French exchange. Private Robinson promptly improved upon this idea. He found a discarded French kepi, put it on his head, and looked over the parapet. He only stayed up for a second or two and ducked again, just as a bullet whizzed over the parapet. He repeated the performance at intervals from different parts of the trench, but finding that his challenge drew quicker and quicker replies was obliged at last to lift the cap no more than into sight on the point of a bayonet. He was rather pleased with the applause of his fellows and the half-dozen prompt bullets which each appearance of the cap at last drew, until one bullet, piercing the cap and striking the point of the bayonet, jarred his fingers unpleasantly and deflected the bullet dangerously and noisily close to his ear. Some of the Frenchmen who were filing out had paused to watch this performance, laughing and bravo-ing at its finish. Robinson bowed with a magnificent flourish, then replaced the kepi on the point of the bayonet, raised the kepi, and made the bayonet bow to the audience. A French officer came bustling along the trench urging his men to move on. He stood there to keep the file passing along without check, and Robinson turned presently to some of the others and asked if they knew what was the meaning of this "Mays ongfong" that the officer kept repeating to his men. "Ongfong," said 'Enery Irving briskly, seizing the opportu-nity to reestablish himself as a French speaker, "means 'children'; spelled e-n-f-a-n-t-s, pronounced *ongfong*."

"Children!" said Robinson. "Infants, eh? 'ealthy lookin' lot o' infants. There's one now - that six-foot chap with the Father Christmas whiskers; 'ow's that for a' infant?"

As the Frenchmen filed out some of them smiled and nodded and called cheery good-bys to our men, and 'Enery Irving turned to a man beside him. "This," he said, "is about where some appropriate music should come in the book. Exit to triumphant strains of martial music Buck up, Snapper! Can't you mouth-organ 'em the Mar-shall-aise?"

Snapper promptly produced his instrument and mouth-organed the opening bars, and the Towers joined in and sang the tune with vociferous "la-la-las." When they had finished, two or three of the Frenchmen, after a quick word together struck up "God Save the King." Instantly the others commenced to pick it up, but before they had sung three words 'Enery Irving, in tones of horror, demanded "The Mar-shall-aise again; quick, you idiot!" from Snapper, and himself swung off into a falsetto rendering of "Three Blind Mice." In a moment the Towers had in full swing their medley caricature of the French march singing, under which "God Save the King" was very completely drowned.

"What the devil d'you mean? Are you all mad?" demanded a wrathful subaltern, plunging round the traverse to where Snapper mouth-organed the "Marseillaise," 'Enery Irving lustily intoned his anthem of the Blind Mice, and Corporal Flannigan passed from the deep lowing of a cow to the clarion calls of the farmyard rooster.

"Beg pardon, sir," said 'Enery Irving with lofty dignity, "but if I 'adn't started this row the 'ole trenchful o' Frenchies would 'ave been 'owling our 'Gawd Save.' I saw that 'ud be a clean give-away, an' the order bein' to act so as to deceive -"

"Quite right," said the officer, "and a smart idea of yours to block it. But who was the crazy ass who started it by singing the 'Marseillaise'?" On this point, however, 'Enery was discreetly silent.

Before the French had cleared the trench the Germans opened a leisurely bombardment with a trench mortar. This delayed the proceeding somewhat, because it was reckoned wiser to halt the men and clear them from the crowded trench into the dug-outs. "With the double company of French and British, there was rather a tight squeeze in the shelters, wonderfully commodious as they were.

"Now this," said Corporal Flannigan, "is what I call something like a dug-out." He looked appreciatively round the square, smooth-walled chamber and up the steps to the small opening which gave admittance to it. "Good dodge, too, this sinking it deep underground. Even if a bomb dropped in the trench just outside, and pieces blew in the door, they'd only go over our heads. Something like, this is."

"I wonder," said another reflectively, "why we don't have dug-outs like this in our line?" He spoke in a slightly aggrieved tone, as if dugouts were things that were issued from the Quarter-Master's store, and therefore a legitimate cause for free complaint. He and his fellows would certainly have felt a good deal more aggrieved, however, if they had been set the labor of making such dug-outs.

Up above, such of the French and British as had been left in the trench were having quite a busy time with the bombs. The Frenchmen had rather a unique way of dodging these, which the Towers were quick to adopt. The whole length of the trench was divided up into compartments by strong traverses running back at right angles from the forward parapet, and in each of these compartments there were anything from four or five to a dozen men, all crowded to the backward end of the traverse, waiting and watching there to see the bomb come twirling slowly and clumsily over. As it reached the highest point of its curve and began to fall down towards the trench, it was as a rule fairly easy to say whether it would fall to right or left of the traverse. If it fell in the trench to the right, the men hurriedly plunged round the corner of the traverse to the left, and waited there till the bomb exploded. The crushing together at the angle of the traverse, the confused cries of warning or advice, or speculation as to which side a bomb would fall, the scuffling, tumbling rush to one side or the other, the cries of derision which greeted the ineffective explosion - all made up a sort of game. The Towers had had a good many unhappy experiences with bombs, and at first played the unknown game carefully and anxiously, and with some doubts as to its results. But they soon picked it up, and presently made quite merry at it, laughing and shouting noisily, tumbling and picking themselves up and laughing again like children.

They lost three men, who were wounded through their slowness in escaping from the compartment where the bomb exploded, and this rather put the Towers on their mettle. As Private Robinson remarked, it wasn't the cheese that a Frenchman should beat an Englishman at any blooming game.

"If we could only get a little bit of a stake on it," he said wistfully, "we could take 'em on, the winners being them that loses least men."

It being impossible, however, to convey to the Frenchmen that interest would be added by the addition of a little bet, the Towers had to content themselves with playing platoon against platoon amongst themselves, the losing platoon pay, what they could conveniently afford, the day's rations of the men who were casualtied. The subsequent task of dividing one and a quarter pots of jam, five portions of cheese, bacon and a meat-and-potato stew was only settled eventually by resource to a set of dice.

As the bombing continued methodically, the French artillery, who were still covering this portion of the trench, set to work to silence the mortar, and the Towers thoroughly enjoyed the ensuing performance, and the generous, not to say extravagant, fashion in which the French battery, after the usual custom of French batteries, lavished its shells upon the task. For five minutes the battery spoke in four-tongued emphatic tones, and the shells screamed over the forward trench, crackled and crashed above the German line, dotted the German parapet along its length, played up and down it in long bursts of fire, and deluged the suspected hiding-place of the mortar with a torrent of high explosive. When it stopped, the bombing also had stopped for that day.

The French infantry did not wait for the ceasing of the artillery fire. They gathered themselves and their belongings and recommenced to move as soon as the guns began to speak.

"Feenish!" as one of them said, placing a finger on the ground, lifting it in a long curve, twirling it over and over and downward again in imitation of a falling bomb. "Ze soixante-quinze speak, bang-bang-bang!" and his fist jerked out four blows in a row. "Feenish!" he concluded, holding a hand out towards the German lines and making a motion of rubbing something off the slate. Plainly they were very proud of their artillery, and the Towers caught that word "soixante-quinze" in every tone of pleasure, pride, and satisfaction. But as Private Robinson said, "I don't wonder at it. Cans is a good name, but can-an'-does would be a better."

When the last of the Frenchmen had gone, the Towers completed their settling in and making themselves comfortable in the vacated quarters. The greatest care was taken to avoid any man showing a British cap or uniform. "Snapper" Brown, urged by the public-spirited 'Enery Irving, exhausted himself in playing the "Marseillaise" at the fullest pitch of his lungs and mouth-organ. His artistic soul revolted at last at the repetition, but since the only other French tune that was suggested was the Blue Danube Waltz, and there appeared to be divergent opinions as to its nationality, "Snapper" at last struck, and refused to play the "Marseillaise" a single time more. 'Enery Irving enthusiastically took up this matter of "acting so as to deceive the Germans."

"Act!" he said. "If I'd a make-up box and a false mustache 'ere, I'd act so as to cheat the French President 'imself, much less a parcel of beer-swilling Germs."

The German trenches were too far away to allow of any conversation, but 'Enery secured a board, wrote on it in large letters "Veev la France," and displayed it over the parapet. After the Germans had signified their notice of the sentiment by firing a dozen shots at it, 'Enery replaced it by a fresh one, "A baa la Bosh." This notice was left standing, but to 'Enery's annoyance the Germans displayed in return a board which said in plain English, "Good morning." "Ain't that a knock out," said 'Enery disgustedly. "Much use me acting to deceive the Germans if some silly blighter in another bit o' the line goes and gives the game away."

Throughout the rest of the day he endeavored to confuse the German's evident information by the display of the French cap and of French sentences on the board like "Bong jewr," "Bong nwee," and "Mercridi," which he told the others was the French for a day of the week, the spelling being correct as he knew because he had seen it written down, and the day indicated, he believed, being Wednesday - or Thursday. "And that's near enough," he said, "because to-day is Wednesday, and if Mercridi means Wednesday, they'll think I'm signaling 'to-day'; and if it means Thursday, they'll think I'm talking about to-morrow." All doubts of the German's knowledge appeared to be removed, however, by their next notice, which stated plainly, "You are Englander." To that 'Enery, his French having failed him, could only retort by a drawing of outstretched fingers and a thumb placed against a prominent nose on an obviously French face, with pointed mustache and imperial, and a French cap. But clearly even this failed, and the German's next message read, "WELL DONE, WALES!" The Towers were annoyed, intensely annoyed, because shortly before that time the strikes of the Welsh miners had been prominent in the English papers, and as the Towers guessed from this notice at least equally prominent in the German journals.

"And I only 'opes," said Robinson, "they sticks that notice up in front of some of the Taffy regiments."

"I don't see that a bit," said 'Enery Irving. "The Taffys out 'ere 'ave done their bit along with the best, and they're just as mad as us, and maybe madder, at these ha'penny-grabbing loafers on strike."

"True enough," said Robinson, "but maybe they'll write 'ome and tell their pals 'ow pleased the Bosche is with them, and 'ave a kind word in passing to say when any of them goes 'ome casualtied or on leave, 'Well done, Wales!' Well, I 'ope Wales likes that smack in the eye," and he spat contemptuously. Presently he had the pleasure of expressing his mind more freely to a French signaler of artillery who was on duty at an observing post in this forward fire trench. The Frenchman had a sufficient smattering of English to ask awkward questions as to why men were allowed to strike in England in war time, but unfortunately not enough to follow Robinson's lengthy and agonized explanations that these men were not English but - a very different thing - Welsh, and, more than that, unpatriotic swine, who ought to be shot. He was reduced at last to turning the unpleasant subject aside by asking what the Frenchman was doing there now the British had taken over. And presently the matter was shelved by a French observing officer, who was on duty there, calling his signalers to attention. The German guns had opened a slow and casual fire about half an hour before on the forward British trench, and now they quickened their fire and commenced methodically to bombard the trench. At his captain's order a signaler called up a battery by telephone. The telephone instrument was in a tall narrow box with a handle at the side, and the signaler ground the handle vigorously for a minute and shouted a long string of hello's into the instrument, rapidly twirled the handle again and shouted, twirled and shouted.

The Towers watched him in some amusement. "'Ere, chum," said Robinson, "you 'aven't put your tuppence in the slot," and 'Enery Irving in a falsetto imitation of a telephone girl's metallic voice drawled: "Put two pennies in, please, and turn the handle after each - one - two - thank you! You're through." The signaler revolved the handle again. "You're mistook, 'Enery," said Robinson, "'e ain't through. Chum, you ought to get your tuppence back."

"Ask to be put through to the inquiry office," said another. "Make a complaint and tell 'em to come and take the blanky thing away if it can't be kept in order. That's what I used to 'ear my governor say every other day."

From his lookout corner the captain called down in rapid French to his signaler.

"D 'ye 'ear that," said Robinson. "Garsong he called him. He's a bloomin' waiter! Well, well, and me thought he was a signaler."

The captain at last was forced to descend from his place, and with the signaler endeavored to rectify the faulty instrument. They got through at last, and the captain spoke to his battery.

"'Ear that," said Robinson. "'Mes on-fong,' he says. He's got a lot o' bloomin' infants too."

"Queer crowd!" said Flannigan. "What with infants for soldiers and a waiter for a signaler, and a butcher or a baker or candlestick-maker for a President, as I'm told they have, they're a rum crush altogether."

The captain ascended to his place again. A German shell, soaring over, burst with a loud *crump* behind the trench. The French signaler laughed and waved derisively towards the shell. He leaned his head and body far to one side, straightened slowly, bent his head on a curve to the other side, and brought it up with a jerk, imitating, as he did so, the sound of the

falling and bursting shell, "*sss-eee-aaa-ahah-aow-Wump.*"
Another shell fell, and "*aow-Wump*," he cried again, shuffling
his feet and laughing gayly. The Towers laughed with him,
and when the next shell fell there was a general chorus of
imitation.

The captain called again, the signaler ground the handle and
spoke into the telephone. "Fire!" he said, nodding delightedly
to the Towers; "boom-boom-boom-boom." Immediately after
they heard the loud, harsh, crackling reports of the battery to
their rear, and the shells rushed whistling overhead.

The signaler mimicked the whistling sound, and clicked his
heels together. "Ha!" he said, "soixante-quinze - good, eh?"
The captain called to him, and again he revolved the handle
and called to the battery.

"Garsong," said Robinson, "a plate of swa-song-canned beans,
si voo play - and serve 'em hot"

A German shell dropped again, and again the chorused howls
and laughter of the Towers marked its fall. The captain called
for high explosive, and the signaler shouted on the order.

"Exploseef," repeated 'Enery Irving, again airing his French.
"That's high explosive."

"Garsong, twopennorth of exploseef soup," chanted Robinson.

Then the order was sent down for rapid fire, and a moment
later the battery burst out in running quadruple reports, and
the shells streamed whistling overhead. The Towers peered
through periscopes and over the parapet to watch the tossing
plumes of smoke and dust that leaped and twisted in the
German lines. "Good old cans!" said Robinson appreciatively.

When the fire stopped, the captain came to the telephone and
spoke to the battery in praise of their shooting. The Towers
listened carefully to catch a word here and there. "There he

goes again," said Robinson, "with 'is bloomin' infants," and later he asked the signaler the meaning of "*mes braves*" that was so often in the captain's mouth.

"'Ear that," he said to the other Towers when the signaler explained it meant "my braves." "Bloomin' braves he's calling his battery now. Infants was bad enough, but 'braves' is about the limit. I'm open to admit they're brave enough; that bombing didn't seem to worry them, and shell-fire pleases them like a call for dinner; and you remember that time we was in action one side of the La Bassee road and they was in it on the other? Strewth! When I remember the wiping they got crossing the open, and the way they stuck it and plugged through that mud, and tore the barbed wire up by the roots, and sailed over into the German trench, I'm not going to contradict anybody that calls 'em brave. But it sounds rum to 'ear 'em call each other it."

Robinson was busy surveying in a periscope the ground between the trenches. "I dunno if I'm seein' things," he remarked suddenly, "but I could 've swore a man's 'and waved out o' the grass over there." With the utmost caution half a dozen men peered out through loopholes and with periscopes in the direction indicated, and presently a chorus of exclamations told that the hand had again been seen. Robinson was just about to wave in reply when 'Enery grabbed his arm.

"You're a nice one to 'act so as to deceive,' you are," he said warmly. "I s'pose a khaki sleeve is likely to make the 'Uns believe we're French. Now, you watch me."

He pulled back his tunic sleeve, held his shirtsleeved arm up the moment the next wave came, and motioned a reply.

"He's in a hole o' some sort," said 'Enery. "Now I wonder who it is. A Frenchie by his tunic sleeve."

"Yes; there's 'is cap," said Robinson suddenly. "Just up - and gone."

"Make the same motion wi' this cap on a bayonet," said 'Enery; "then knock off, case the Boshies spot 'im."

The matter was reported, and presently a couple of officers came along, made a careful examination, and waved the cap. A cautious reply, and a couple of bullets whistling past their cap came at the same moment.

Later, 'Enery sought the sergeant. "Mind you this, sergeant," he said, "if there's any volunteerin' for the job o' fetchin' that chap in, he belongs to me. I found 'im." The sergeant grinned.

"Robinson was here two minutes ago wi' the same tale," he said. "Seems you're all in a great hurry to get shot."

"Like his bloomin' cheek!" said the indignant 'Enery. "I know why he wants to go out; he's after those German helmets the interpreter told us was lyin' out there."

The difficulty was solved presently by the announcement that an officer was going out and would take two volun-teers - B Company to have first offer. 'Enery and Robinson secured the post, and 'Enery immediately sought the officer. Reminding him of the order to "act so as to deceive," he unfolded a plan which was favorably considered.

"Those Boshies thought they was bloomin' clever to twig we was English," he told the others of B Company; "but you wait till the lime-light's on me. I'll puzzle 'em."

The two French artillery signalers were sleeping in the forward trench, and after some explanation readily lent their long-skirted coats. The officer and Robinson donned one each, and 'Enery carefully arrayed himself in a torn and discarded pair of old French baggy red breeches and the damaged French cap, and discarded his own jacket. His gray shirt might have been of any nationality, so that on the whole he made quite a passable Frenchman. While they waited for darkness he paraded the trench, shrugging his shoulders, and gesticulating.

"Bon joor, mays ong-fong," he remarked with a careless hand-wave. "Hey, gar-song! Donney-moi du pang eh du beurre, si voo play - and donnay-moi swoy-song cans - rapeed - exploseef! Merci, mes braves, mes bloomin' 'eroes ... mes noble warriors, merci. Snapper, strike up the 'Conkerin' 'Ero,' if you please."

Before the time came to go he added to his make-up by marking on his face with a burnt stick huge black mustachios and an imperial, and although the officer stared a little when he came along he ended by laughing, and leaving 'Enery his "make-up" disguise.

An hour after dark the three slipped quietly over the parapet and out through the barbed wire, dragging a stretcher after them. It was a fairly quiet night, with only an occasional rifle cracking and no artillery fire. A bright moon floated behind scudding clouds, and perhaps helped the adventure by the alternate minutes of light and dark and the difficulty of focusing eyes to the differences of moonlight and dark and the blaze of an occasional flare when the moon was obscured. Behind the parapet the Towers waited with rifles ready, and stared out through the loopholes; and behind them the French artillery officer, and his signalers standing by their telephone, also waited with the loaded guns and ready gunners at the other end of the wire. The watchers saw the dark blot of men and stretcher slip under the wires, and slowly, very slowly, creep on through the long grass. Half-way across, the watchers lost them amidst the other black blots and shadows, and it was a full half-hour after when a private exclaimed suddenly: "I see them," he said. "There, close where we saw the hand."

The moon vanished a moment, then sailed clear, throwing a strong silvery light across the open ground, and showing plainly the German wire entanglements and the black-and-white patchwork of their barricade. There were no visible signs of the rescue party, for the good reason that they had slipped into and lay prone in the wide shell crater that held the wounded Frenchman. Far spent the man was when they found him, for he had lain there three nights and two days with a bullet-smashed thigh and the scrape across his skull that had led the rest of his night patrol to count him dead and so abandon him.

Now the moon slid again behind the racing clouds, and patches of light and shadow in turn chased across the open ground.

"Here they come," said the captain of B Company a few minutes later. "At least I think it's them, altho' I can only see two men and no stretcher."

"Do you see them?" said an eager voice in French at his ear, and when he turned and found the gunner captain and explained to him, the captain made a gesture of despair. "Perhaps it is that they cannot move him," he said. "Or would they, do you think, return for more help? I should go myself but that I may be needed to talk with the battery. Perhaps one of my signalers -"

But the Englishman assured him it was better to wait; they could not be returning for help; that the three could do all a dozen could.

Again they waited and watched in eager suspense, glimpsing the crawling figures now and then, losing them again, in doubts and certainty in swift turns as to the whereabouts and identity of the crawling figures.

"There is one of them," said the captain quickly; "there, by himself, in those cursed red breeches. They show up in the flarelight like a blood-spot on a clean collar. Dashed idiot! And I was a fool, too, to let him go like that."

But it was plain now that 'Enery Irving was dragging his red breeches well clear of the others, although it was not plain, what the others had done with the stretcher. There were two of them at the length of a stretcher apart, and yet no visible stretcher lay between them. It was the sergeant who solved the mystery.

"I'm blowed!" he said, in admiring wonder; "they've covered the stretcher over with cut grass. They've got their man too - see his head this end."

Now that they knew it, all could see the outline of the man's body covered over with grass, the thick tufts waving upright from his hands and nodding between his legs.

They were three-quarters of the way across now, but still with a dangerous slope to cross. It was ever so slight, but, tilted as it was towards the enemy's line, it was enough to show much more plainly anything that moved or lay upon its face. They crawled on with a slowness that was an agony to watch, crawled an inch at a time, lying dead and still when a light flared, hitching themselves and the dragging stretcher onwards as the dullness of hazed moonlight fell.

The French captain was consumed with impatience, muttering exhortations to caution, whispering excited urgings to move, as if his lips were at the creepers' ears, his fingers twitching and jerking, his body hitching and holding still, exactly as if he too crawled out there and dragged at the stretcher.

And then when it seemed that the worst was over, when there was no more than a score of feet to cover to the barbed wire, when they were actually crawling over the brow of the gentle rise, discovery came. There were quick shots from one spot of the German parapet, confused shouting, the upward soaring of half a dozen blazing flares.

And then before the two dragging the stretcher could move in a last desperate rush for safety, before they could rise from their prone position, they heard the rattle of fire increase swiftly to a trembling staccato roar. But, miracu-lously, no bullets came near them, no whistling was about their ears, no ping and smack of impacting lead hailed about them - except, yes, just the fire of one rifle or two that sent aimed bullet after bullet hissing over them. They could not understand it, but without waiting to understand they half rose, thrust and hauled at the stretcher, dragged it under the wires, heaved it over to where eager hands tore down the sandbags to gap a passage for them. A handful of bullets whipped and rapped about them as they tumbled over, and the stretcher was hoisted in, but nothing worth mention, nothing certainly of that volume of fire that drammed and rolled out over there. They did not under-stand; but the others in the trench understood, and laughed a little and swore a deal, then shut their teeth and set themselves to pump bullets in a covering fire upon the German parapet.

The stretcher party drew little or no fire, simply and solely because just one second after those first shots and loud shouts had declared the game up, a figure sprang from the grass fifty yards along the trench and twice as far out in the open, sprang up and ran out, and stood in the glare of light, the baggy scarlet breeches and gray shirt making a flaring mark that no eye, called suddenly to see, could miss, that no rifle brought sliding through the loophole and searching for a target could fail to mark. The bullets began to patter about 'Enery Irving's feet, to whine and whimper and buzz about his ears. And 'Enery - this was where the trench, despite themselves, laughed - 'Enery placed his hand on his heart, swept off his cap in a magnificent arm's length gesture, and bowed low; then swiftly he rose upright, struck an attitude that would have graced the hero of the highest class Adelphi drama, and in a shrill voice that rang clear above the hammering tumult of the rifles, screamed "Veev la France! A baa la Bosh!" The rifles by this time were pelting a storm of lead at him, and now that the haste and flurry of the urgent call had passed and the shooters had steadied to their task, the storm was perilously close. 'Enery stayed a moment even then to spread his hands and raise his shoulders ear-high in a magnificent stage shrug; but a bullet snatched the cap from his head, and 'Enery ducked hastily, turned, and ran his hardest, with the bullets snapping at his heels.

Back in the trench a frantic French captain was raving at the telephone, whirling the handle round, screaming for "Fire, fire, fire!"

Private Flannigan looked over his shoulder at him, "Mong capitaine," he said, "you ought, you reely ought, to ring up your telephone; turn the handle round an' say something."

"Drop two pennies in," mocked another as the captain birr-r-red the handle and yelled again.

Whether he got through, or whether the burst of rifle fire reached the listening ears at the guns, nobody knew; but just as 'Enery did his ear-embracing shoulder-shrug the first shells screamed over, burst and leaped down along the German parapet. After that there was no complaint about the guns. They scourged the parapet from end to end, up and down, and up again; they shook it with the blast of high explosive, ripped and flayed it with, driving blasts of shrapnel, smothered it with a tempest of fire and lead, blotted it out behind a veil of writhing smoke.

At the sound of the first shot the gunner captain had leaped back to the trench. "Is he in? Is he arrived?" he shouted in the ear of the B Company captain who leaned anxiously over the parapet. The captain drew back and down. "He's in - bless him - I mean dash his impudent hide!"

The Frenchman turned and called to his signaler, and the next moment the guns ceased. But the captain waited, watching with narrowed eyes the German parapet. The storm of his shells had obliterated the rifle fire, but after a few minutes it opened up again in straggling shots.

The captain snapped back a few orders, and prompt to his word the shells leaped and struck down again on the parapet. A dozen rounds and they ceased, and again the captain waited and watched. The rifles were silent now, and presently the captain relaxed his scowling glare and his tightened lips.

"Vermin!" he said. He used just the tone a man gives to a ferocious dog he has beaten and cowed to a sullen submission.

But he caught sight of 'Enery making his way along the trench past his laughing and chaffing mates, and leaped down and ran to him. "Bravo!" he beamed, and threw his arms round the astonished soldier, and before he could dodge, as the disgusted 'Enery said afterwards, "planted two quick-fire kisses, smack, smack," on his two cheeks.

"*Mon brave!*" he said, stepping back and regarding 'Enery with shining eyes, "*Mon brave, mon beau Anglais, mon -*"

But 'Enery's own captain arrived here and interrupted the flow of admiration, cursing the grinning and sheepish private for a this, that, and the other crazy, play-acting idiot, and winding up abruptly by shaking hands with him and saying gruffly, "Good work, though. B Company's proud of you, and so'm I."

"An' I admit I felt easier after that rough-tonguin'," 'Enery told B Company that night over a mess-tin of tea. "It was sort of natural-like, an' what a man looks for, and it broke up about as unpleasant a sit-u-ation as I've seen staged. I could see you all grinnin', and I don't wonder at it. That slobberin' an' kissin' business, an' the Mong Brav Conkerin' 'Ero may be all right for a lot o' bloomin' Frenchies that don't know better -"

He took a long swig of tea.

"Though, mind you," he resumed, "I haven't a bad word to fit to a Frenchman. They're real good fighting stuff, an' they ain't arf the light-'earted an' light-'eaded grinnin' giddy goats I used to take 'em for."

"There wasn't much o' the light 'eart look about the Mong Cappytaine to-night," said Robinson. "'Is eyes was snappin' like two ends o' a live wire, and 'e 'andled them guns as business-like as a butcher cutting chops."

"That's it," said 'Enery, "business-like is the word for 'em. I noticed them 'airy-faces shootin' to-day. They did it like they was sent there to kill somebody, and they meant doin' their job thorough an' competent. Afore I come this trip on the Continong I used to think a Frenchman was good for nothing but fiddlin' an' dancin' an' makin' love. But since I've seen 'em settin' to Bosh partners an' dancin' across the neutral ground an' love-makin' wi' Rosalie,[Footnote: *Rosalie* - the French nickname for the bayonet.] I've learned better. 'Ere's luck to 'im," and he drained the mess-tin.

And the French, if one might judge from the story *mon capitaine* had to tell his major, had also revised some ancient opinions of their Allies.

"Cold!" he said scornfully; "never again tell me these English are cold. Children - perhaps. Foolish - but yes, a little. They try to kill a man between jests; they laugh if a bullet wounds a comrade so that he grimaces with pain - it is true; I saw it." It *was* true, and had reference to a sight scrape of a bullet across the tip of the nose of a Towers private, and the ribald jests and laughter thereat. "They make jokes, and say a man 'stopped one,' meaning a shell had been stopped in its flight by exploding on him - this the interpreter has explained to me. But cold - no, no, no! If you had seen this man - ah, sublime, magnificent! With the whistling balls all round him he stands, so brave, so noble, so fine, stands - so! '*Vive la France!*' he cried aloud, with a tongue of trumpets; '*Vive la France! A bas les Boches!*'"

The captain, as he declaimed "with a tongue of trumpets," leaped to his feet and struck an attitude that was really quite a good imitation of 'Enery's own mock-tragedian one. But the officers listening breathed awe and admiration; they did not, as the Towers did, laugh, because here, unlike the Towers, they saw nothing to laugh at.

The captain dropped to his chair amid a murmur of applause. "Sublime!" he said. "That posture, that cry! Indeed, it was worthy of a Frenchman. But certainly we must recommend him for a Cross of France, eh, my major?"

'Enery Irving got the Cross of the Legion of Honor. But I doubt if it ever gave him such pure and legitimate joy as did a notice stuck up in the German trench next day. Certainly it insulted the English by stating that their workers stayed at home and went on strike while Frenchmen fought and died. *But* it was headed "Frenchman!" *and it was written in French.*

THE FEAR OF FEAR

"At - we recaptured the portion of front line trench lost by us some days ago." - EXTRACT FROM DISPATCH.

"In a charge," said the Sergeant, "the 'Hotwater Guards' don't think about going back till there's none of them left to go back; and you can always remember this: if you go forward you *may* die, if you go back you *will* die."

The memory of that phrase came back to Private Everton, tramping down the dark road to the firing-line. Just because he had no knowledge of how he himself would behave in this his baptism of fire, just because he was in deadly fear that he would feel fear, or, still worse, show it, he strove to fix that phrase firmly in front of his mind. "If I can remember that," he thought, "it will stop me going back, anyway," and he repeated: "If you go back you *will* die, if you go back you *will* die," over and over.

It is true that, for all his repetition, when a field battery, hidden close by the side of the road on which they marched, roared in a sudden and ear-splitting salvo of six guns, for the instant he thought he was under fire and that a huge shell had burst somewhere desperately close to them. He had jumped, his comrades assured him afterwards, a clear foot and a half off the ground, and he himself remembered that his first involuntary glance and thought flashed to the deep ditch that ran alongside the road.

When he came to the trenches, at last, and filed down the narrow communication-trench and into his Company's

BOYD CABLE

appointed position in the deep ditch with a narrow platform along its front that was the forward fire-trench, he remembered with unpleasant clearness that instinctive start and thought of taking cover. By that time he had actually been under fire, had heard the shells rush over him and the shattering noise of their burst; had heard the bullets piping and humming and hissing over the communication - and firing-trenches. He took a little comfort from the fact that he had not felt any great fear then, but he had to temper that by the admission that there was little to be afraid of there in the shelter of the deep trench. It was what he would do and feel when he climbed out of cover on to the exposed and bullet-swept flat before the trench that he was in doubt about; for the Hotwaters had been told that at nine o'clock there was to be a brief but intense bombardment on a section of trench in front of them which had been captured from us the day before, and which, after several counter-attacks had failed, was to be taken that morning by this battalion of Hotwaters.

At half-past eight, nobody entering their trench would have dreamed that the Hotwaters were going into a serious action in half an hour. The men were lounging about, squatting on the firing-step, chaffing and talking - laughing even - quite easily and naturally; some were smoking, and others had produced biscuits and bully beef from their haversacks and were calmly eating their breakfast.

Everton felt a glow of pride as he looked at them. These men were his friends, his fellows, his comrades: they were of the Hotwater Guards - his regiment, and his battalion. He had heard often enough that the Guards Brigades were the finest brigades in the Army, that this particular brigade was the best of all the Guards, that his battalion was the best of the Brigade. Hitherto he had rather deprecated these remarks as savoring of pride and self-conceit, but now he began to believe that they must be true; and so believing, if he had but known it, he had taken another long step on the way to becoming the perfect soldier, who firmly believes his regiment the finest in the world and is ready to die in proof of the belief.

"Dusty Miller," the next file on his left, who was eating bread and cheese, spoke to him.

"Why don't you eat some grab, Toffee?" he mumbled cheerfully, with his mouth full. "In a game like this you never know when you'll get the next chance of a bite."

"Don't feel particularly hungry," answered Toffee with an attempt to appear as off-handed and casual and at ease as his questioner. "So I think I'd better save my ration until I'm hungry."

Dusty Miller sliced off a wedge of bread with the knife edge against his thumb, popped it in his mouth, and followed it with a corner of cheese.

"A-ah!" he said profoundly, and still munching; "there's no sense in saving rations when you're going into action. I'd a chum once that always did that; said he got more satisfaction out of a meal when the job was over and he was real hungry, and had a chance to eat in comfort - more or less comfort. And one day we was for it he saved a tin o' sardines and a big chunk of cake and a bottle of pickled onions that had just come to him from home the day before; said he was looking forward to a good feed that night after the show was over. And - and he was killed that day!"

Dusty Miller halted there with the inborn artistry that left his climax to speak for itself.

"Hard luck!" said Toffee sympathetically. "So his feed was wasted!"

"Not to say wasted exactly," said Dusty, resuming bread and cheese. "Because I remembers to this day how good them onions was. Still it was wasted, far as he was concerned - and he was particular fond o' pickled onions."

But even the prospect of wasting his rations did nothing to

induce Toffee to eat a meal. The man on Toffee's right was crouched back on the firing-step apparently asleep or near it. Dusty Miller had turned and opened a low-toned conversation with the next man, the frequent repetition of "I says" and "she says" affording some clew to the thread of his story and inclining Toffee to believe it not meant for him to hear. He felt he must speak to some one, and it was with relief that he saw Halliday, the man on his other side, rouse himself and look up. Something about Toffee's face caught his attention.

"How are you feeling?" he asked, leaning forward and speaking quietly. "This is your first charge, isn't it!"

"Yes," said Toffee, "I'm all right. I - I think I'm all right."

The other moved slightly on the firing-step, leaving a little room, and Toffee took this as an invitation to sit down. Halliday continued to speak in low tones that were not likely to pass beyond his listener's ear.

"Don't you get scared," he said. "You've nothing much to be scared about."

He threw a little emphasis, and Toffee fancied a little envy, into the "you."

"I'm not scared exactly," said Toffee. "I'm sort of wonde-ring what it will be like."

"I know," said Halliday, "I know; and who should, if I didn't? But I can tell you this - you don't need to be afraid of shells, you don't need to be afraid of bullets, and least of all is there any need to be afraid of the cold iron when the Hotwaters get into the trench. You don't need to be afraid of being wounded, because that only means home and a hospital and a warm dry bed; you don't need to be afraid of dying, because you've got to die some day, anyhow. There's only one thing in this game to be afraid of, and there isn't many finds that in their first engagement. It's the ones like me that get it."

Toffee glanced at him curiously and in some amazement. Now that he looked closely, he could see that, despite his easy loungeful attitude and steady voice, and apparently indifferent look, there was something odd and unexplainable about Halliday: some faintest twitching of his lips, a shade of pallor on his cheek, a hunted look deep at the back of his eyes. Everton tried to speak lightly.

"And what is it, then, that the likes o' you get?"

Halliday's voice sank to little more than a whisper. "It's the fear o' fear," he said steadily. "Maybe, you think you know what that is, that you feel it yourself. You know what I mean, I suppose?"

Toffee nodded. "I think so," he said. "What I fear myself is that I'll be afraid and show that I'm afraid, that I'll do something rotten when we get out up there."

He jerked his head up and back towards the open where the rifles sputtered and the bullets whistled querulously.

"There's plenty fear that," admitted Halliday, "before their first action; but mostly it passes the second they leave cover and can't protect themselves and have to trust to whatever there is outside, themselves to bring them through. You don't know the beginning of how bad the fear o' fear can be till you have seen dozens of your mates killed, till you've had death no more than touch you scores of times, like I have."

"But you don't mean to tell me," said Toffee incredulously, "that you are afraid of yourself, that you can't trust yourself now? Why, I've heard said often that you're one of the coolest under fire, and that you don't know what fear is!"

"It's a good reputation to have if you can keep it," said Halliday. "But it makes it worse if you can't."

"I wish," said Toffee enviously, "I was as sure of keeping it as you are to-day."

Halliday pulled his hand from his pocket and held it beside him where only Toffee could see it. It was quivering like a flag-halliard in a stiff breeze. He thrust it back in his pocket.

"Doesn't look too sure, does it?" he said grimly. "And my heart is shaking a sight worse than my hand."

He was interrupted by the arrival of a group of German shells on and about the section of trench they were in. One burst on the rear lip of the trench, spattering earth and bullets about them and leaving a choking reek swirling and eddying along the trench. There was silence for an instant, and then an officer's voice called from the near traverse. "Is anybody hit there!" A sergeant shouted back "No, sir," and was immediately remonstrated with by an indignant private busily engaged in scraping the remains of a mud clod from his eye.

"You might wait a minute, Sergeant," he said, "afore you reports no casualties, just to give us time to look round and count if all our limbs is left on. And I've serious doubts at this minute whether my eye is in its right place or bulging out the back o' my head; anyway, it feels as if an eight-inch Krupp had bumped fair into it."

When the explosion came, Toffee Everton had instinctively ducked and crouched, but he noticed that Halliday never moved or gave a sign of the nearness of any danger. Toffee remarked this to him.

"And I don't see," he confessed, "where that fits in with this hand - and heart-shaking o' yours."

Halliday looked at him curiously.

"If that was the worst," he said, "I could stand it. It isn't. It isn't the beginning of the least of the worst. If it had fell in the trench, now, and mucked up half a dozen men, there'd have been something to squeal about. That's the sort o' thing that breaks a man up - your own mates that was talking to you a minute afore, ripped to bits and torn to ribbons. I've seen nothing left of a whole live man but a pair o' burnt boots. I've seen -" He stopped abruptly and shivered a little. "I'm not going to talk about it," he said. "I think about it and see it too often in my dreams as it is. And, besides," he went on, "I didn't duck that time, because I've learnt enough to know it's too late to duck when the shell bursts a dozen yards from you. I'm not so much afraid of dying, either. I've got to die, I've little doubt, before this war is out; I don't think there's a dozen men in this battalion that came out with it in the beginning and haven't been home sick or wounded since. I've seen one-half the battalion wiped out in one engagement and built up with drafts, and the other half wiped out in the next scrap. We've lost fifty and sixty and seventy per cent. of our strength at different times, and I've come through it all without a scratch. Do you suppose I don't know it's against reason for me to last out much longer? But I'm not afraid o' that. I'm not afraid of the worst death I've seen a man die - and that's something pretty bad, believe me. What I'm afraid of is myself, of my nerve cracking, of my doing something that will disgrace the Regiment."

The man's nerves were working now; there was a quiver of excitement in his voice, a grayer shade on his cheek, a narrowing and a restless movement of his eyes, a stronger twitching of his lips. More shells crashed sharply; a little along the line a gust of rifle-bullets swept over and into the parapet; a Maxim rap-rap-rapped and its bullets spat hailing along the parapet above their heads.

Halliday caught his breath and shivered again.

"That," he said - "that is one of the devils we've got to face presently." His eyes glanced furtively about him. "God!" he muttered, "if I could only get out of this! 'Tisn't fair, I tell ye, it isn't fair to ask a man that's been through what I have to take it on again, knowing that if I do come through, 'twill be the same thing to go through over and over until they get me; or until my own sergeant shoots me for refusing to face it."

Everton had listened in amazed silence - an understanding utterly beyond him. He knew the name that Halliday bore in the regiment, knew that he was seeing and hearing more than Halliday perhaps had ever shown or told to anyone. Shame-facedly and self-consciously, he tried to say something to console and hearten the other man, but Halliday interrupted him roughly.

"That's it!" he said bitterly. "Go on! Pat me on the back and tell me to be a good boy and not to be frightened. I'm coming to it at last: old Bob Halliday that's been through it from the beginning, one o' the Old Contemptibles, come down to be mothered and hushaby-baby'd by a blanky recruit, with the first polish hardly off his new buttons."

He broke off and into bitter cursing, reviling the Germans, the war, himself and Everton, his sergeant and platoon commander, the O.C., and at last the regiment itself. But at that the torrent of his oaths broke off, and he sat silent and shaking for a minute. He glanced sideways at last at the embarrassed Everton.

"Don't take no notice o' me, chum," he said. "I wasn't speaking too loud, was I? The others haven't noticed, do you think? I don't want to look round for a minute."

Everton assured him that he had not spoken too loud, that nobody appeared to have noticed anything, and that none were looking their way. He added a feeble question as to whether Halliday, if he felt so bad, could not report himself as sick or something and escape having to leave the trench.

Halliday's lips twisted in a bitter grin.

"That would be a pretty tale," he said. "No, boy, I'll try and pull through once more, and if my heart fails me - look here,

I've often thought o' this, and some day, maybe, it will come to it."

He lifted his rifle and put the butt down in the trench bottom, slipped his bayonet out, and holding the rifle near the muzzle with one hand, with the other placed the point of the bayonet to the trigger of the rifle. He removed it instantly and returned it to its place.

"There's always that," he said. "It can be done in a second, and no matter how a man's hand shakes, he can steady the point of the bayonet against the trigger-guard, push it down till the point pushes the trigger home."

"Do you mean," stammered Everton in amazement - "do you mean - shoot yourself?"

"Ssh! not so loud," cautioned Halliday. "Yes, it's better than being shot by my own officer, isn't it?"

Everton's mind was floundering hopelessly round this strange problem. He could understand a man being afraid; he was not sure that he wasn't afraid himself; but that a man afraid that he could not face death could yet contemplate certain death by his own hand, was completely beyond him.

Halliday drew his breath in a deep sigh.

"We'll say no more about it," he said. "I feel better now; it's something to know I always have that to fall back on at the worst. I'll be all right now - until it comes the minute to climb over the parapet."

It was nearly nine o'clock, and word was passed down the line for every man to get down as low as he could in the bottom of the trench. The trench they were about to attack was only forty or fifty yards away, and since the Heavies as well as the Field guns were to bombard, there was quite a large possibility of splinters and fragments being thrown by the lyddite back as far as the British trench. At nine, sharp to the tick of the clock, the *rush, rush, rush* of a field battery's shells passed overhead. Because the target was so close, the passing shells seemed desperately near to the British parapet, as indeed they actually were. The rush of shells and the crash of their explosion sounded in the forward trench before the boom of the guns which fired them traveled to the British trench. Before the first round of this opening battery had finished, another and another joined in, and then, in a deluge of noise, the intense bombardment commenced.

Crouching low in the bottom of the trench, half deafened by the uproar, the men waited for the word to move. The concentrated fire on this portion of front indicated clearly to the Germans that an attack was coming, and where it was to be expected. The obviously correct procedure for the gunners was of course to have bombarded many sections of front so that no certain clew would be given as to the point of the coming attack. But this was in the days when shells were very, very precious things, and gunners had to grit their teeth helplessly, doling out round by round, while the German gun- and rifle-fire did its worst. The Germans, then, could see now where the attack was concentrated, and promptly proceeded to break it up before it was launched. Shells began to sweep the trench where the Hotwater Guards lay, to batter at their parapet, and to prepare a curtain of fire along their front.

Everton lay and listened to the appalling clamor; but when the word was passed round to get ready, he rose to his feet and climbed to the firing-step without any overpowering sense of fear. A sentence from the man on his left had done a good deal to hearten him.

"Gostrewth! 'ark at our guns!" he said. "They ain't 'arf pitchin' it in. W'y, this ain't goin' to be no charge; it's going to be a sort of merry picnic, a game of ''Ere we go gatherin' nuts in May.' There won't be any Germans left in them trenches, and we'll 'ave nothin' to do but collect the 'elmets and sooveneers and make ourselves at 'ome."

"Did you hear that!" Everton asked Halliday. "Is it anyways true, do you think?"

"A good bit," said Halliday. "I've never seen a bit of German front smothered up by our guns the way this seems to be now, though I've often enough seen it the other way. The trench in front should be smashed past any shape for stopping our charge if the gunners are making any straight shooting at all."

It was evident that the whole trench shared his opinion, and expressions of amazed delight ran up and down the length of the Hotwaters. When the order came to leave the trench, the men were up and out of it with a bound.

Everton was too busy with his own scramble put to pay much heed to Halliday; but as they worked out through their own barbed wire, he was relieved to find him at his side. He caught Everton's look, and although his teeth were gripped tight, he nodded cheerfully. Presently, when they were forming into line again beyond the wire, Halliday spoke.

"Not too bad," he said. "The guns has done it for us this time. Come on, now, and keep your wits when you get across."

In the ensuing rush across the open, Everton was conscious of no sensation of fear. The guns had lifted their fire farther back as the Hotwaters emerged from their trench, and the rush and rumble of their shells was still passing overhead as the line advanced. The German artillery hardly dared drop their range to sweep the advance, because of its proximity to their own trench. A fairly heavy rifle-fire was coming from the flanks, but to a certain extent that was kept down by some of our batteries spreading their fire over those portions of the German trench which were not being attacked, and by a heavy rifle-and-machine-gun fire which was pelted across from the opposite parts of the British line.

From the immediate front, which was the Hotwaters' objective, there was practically no attempt at resistance until the advance was half-way across the short distance between the trenches, and even then it was no more than a spasmodic attempt and the feeble resistance of a few rifles and a machine-gun. The Hotwaters reached the trench with comparatively slight loss, pushed into it, and over it, and pressed on to the next line, the object being to threaten the continuance of the attack, to take the next trench if the resistance was not too severe, and so to give time for the reorganization of the first captured trench to resist the German counter-attack.

Everton was one of the first to reach the forward trench. It had been roughly handled by the artillery fire, and the men in it made little show of resistance. The Hotwaters swarmed into the broken ditch, shooting and stabbing the few who fought back, disarming the prisoners who had surrendered with hands over their heads and quavering cries of "Kamerad." Everton rushed one man who appeared to be in two minds whether to surrender or not, fingering and half lifting his rifle and lowering it again, looking round over his shoulder, once more raising his rifle muzzle. Everton killed him with the bayonet. Afterwards he climbed out and ran on, after the line had pushed forward to the next trench. There was an awe, and a thrill of satisfaction in his heart as he looked at his stained bayonet, but, as he suddenly recognized with a tremendous joy, not the faintest sensation of being afraid. He looked round grinning to the man next him, and was on the point of shouting some jest to him, when he saw the man stumble and pitch heavily on his face. It flashed into Everton's mind that he had tripped over a hidden wire, and he was about to shout some chaffing remark, when he saw the back of the man's head as he lay face down. But even that unpleasant sight brought no fear to him.

There was a stout barricade of wire in front of the next trench, and an order was shouted along to halt and lie down in front of it. The line dropped, and while some lay prone and fired as fast as they could at any loophole or bobbing head they could see, others lit bombs and tossed them into the trench. This trench also had been badly mauled by the shells, and the fire from it was feeble. Everton lay firing for a few minutes, casting side glances on an officer close in front of him, and on two or three men along the line who were coolly cutting through the barbed wire with heavy nippers. Everton saw the officer spin round and drop to his knees, his left hand nursing his hanging right arm. Everton jumped up and went over to him.

"Let me go on with it, sir," he said eagerly, and without waiting for any consent stooped and picked up the fallen wire-cutters and set to work. He and the others, standing erect and working on the wire, naturally drew a heavy proportion of the aimed fire; but Everton was only conscious of an uplifting exhilaration, a delight that he should have had the chance at such a prominent position. Many bullets came very close to him, but none touched him, and he went on cutting wire after wire, quickly and methodically, grasping the strand well in the jaws of the nippers, gripping till the wire parted and the severed ends sprang loose, calmly fitting the nippers to the next strand.

Even when he had cut a clear path through, he went on working, widening the breach, cutting more wires, dragging the trailing ends clear. Then he ran back to the line and to the officer who had lain watching him.

"Your wire-nippers, sir," he said. "Shall I put them in your case for you?"

"Stick them in your pocket, Everton," said the youngster; "you've done good work with them. Now lie down here."

All this was a matter of no more than three or four minutes' work. When the other gaps were completed - the men in them being less fortunate than Everton and having several wounded during the task - the line rose, rushed streaming through the gaps and down into the trench. If anything, the damage done by the shells was greater there than in the first line, mainly perhaps because the heavier guns had not hesitated to fire on the second line where the closeness of the first line to the

　　　　　　BOYD CABLE

British would have made risky shooting. There were a good many dead and wounded Germans in this second trench, and of the remainder many were hidden away in their dug-outs, their nerves shaken beyond the sticking-point of courage by the artillery fire first, and later by the close-quarter bombing and the rush of the cold steel.

The Hotwaters held that trench for some fifteen minutes. Then a weak counter-attack attempted to emerge from another line of trenches a good two hundred yards back, but was instantly fallen upon by our artillery and scourged by the accurate fire of the Hotwaters. The attack broke before it was well under way, and scrambled back under cover.

Shortly afterwards the first captured trench having been put into some shape for defense, the advance line of the Hotwaters retired. A small covering party stayed and kept up a rapid fire till most of the others had gone, and then climbed through the trench and doubled back after them.

The officer, whose wire-cutters Everton had used, had been hit rather badly in the arm. He had made light of the wound, and remained in the trench with the covering party; but when he came to retire, he found that the pain and loss of blood had left him shaky and dizzy. Everton helped him to climb from the trench; but as they ran back he saw from the corner of his eye that the officer had slowed to a walk. He turned back and, ignoring the officer's advice to push on, urged him to lean on him. It ended up by Everton and the officer being the last men in, Everton half supporting, half carrying the other. Once more he felt a childish pleasure at this opportunity to distinguish himself. He was half intoxicated with the heady wine of excitement and success, he asked only for other and greater and riskier opportunities. "Risk," he thought contemptuously, "is only a pleasant excitement, danger the spice to the risk." He asked his sergeant to be allowed to go out and help the stretcher-bearers who were clearing the wounded from the ground over which the first advance had been made.

"No," said the Sergeant shortly. "The stretcher-bearers have their job, and they've got to do it. Your job is here, and you can stop and do that. You've done enough for one day." Then, conscious perhaps that he had spoken with unnecessary sharpness, he added a word. "You've made a good beginning, lad, and done good work for your first show; don't spoil it with rank gallery play."

But now that the German gunners knew the British line had advanced and held the captured trench, they pelted it, the open ground behind it, and the trench that had been the British front line, with a storm of shell-fire. The rifle-fire was hotter, too, and the rallied defense was pouring in whistling stream of bullets. But the captured trench, which it will be remembered was a recaptured British one, ran back and joined up with the British lines. It was possible therefore to bring up plenty of ammunition, sandbags, and reinforcements, and by now the defense had been sufficiently made good to have every prospect of resisting any counter-attack and of with-standing the bombardment to which it was being subjected. But the heavy fire drove the stretcher-bearers off the open ground, while there still remained some dead and wounded to be brought in.

Everton had missed Halliday, and his anxious inquiries failed to find him or any word of him, until at last one man said he believed Halliday had been dropped in the rush on the first trench. Everton stood up and peered back over the ground behind them. Thirty yards away he saw a man lying prone and busily at work with his trenching-tool, endeavoring to build up a scanty cover. Everton shouted at the pitch of his voice, "Halliday!" The digging figure paused, lifted the trenching-tool and waved it, and then fell to work again. Everton pressed along the crowded trench to the sergeant.

"Sergeant," he said breathlessly, "Halliday's lying out there wounded, he's a good pal o' mine and I'd like to fetch him in."

The Sergeant was rather doubtful. He made Everton point

out the digging figure, and was calculating the distance from the nearest point of the trench, and the bullets that drummed between.

"It's almost a cert you get hit," he said, "even if you crawl out. He's got a bit of cover and he's making more, fast. I think -"

A voice behind interrupted, and Everton and the Sergeant turned to find the Captain looking up at them.

"What's this?" he repeated, and the Sergeant explained the position.

"Go ahead!" said the Captain. "Get him in if you can, and good luck to you."

Everton wanted no more. Two minutes later he was out of the trench and racing back across the open.

"Come on, Halliday," he said. "I'll give you a hoist in. Where are you hit?"

"Leg and arm," said Halliday briefly; and then, rather ungraciously, "You're a fool to be out here; but I suppose now you're here, you might as well give me a hand in."

But he spoke differently after Everton had given him a hand, had lifted him and carried him, and so brought him back to the trench and lowered him into waiting hands. His wounds were bandaged and, before he was carried off, he spoke to Everton.

"Good-by, Toffee," he said and held out his left hand, "I owe you a heap. And look here -" He hesitated a moment and then spoke in tones so low that Everton had to bend over the stretcher to hear him. "My leg's smashed bad, and I'm done for the Front and the old Hotwaters. I wouldn't like it to get about - I don't want the others to think - to know about me feeling - well, like I told you back there before the charge."

Toffee grabbed the uninjured-hand hard. "You old frost!" he said gayly, "there's no need to keep it up any longer now; but I don't mind telling you, old man, you fairly hoaxed me that time, and actually I believed what you were saying. 'Course, I know better now; but I'll punch the head off any man that ever whispers a word against you."

Halliday looked at him queerly. "Good-by, Toffee," he said again, "and thank ye."

ANTI-AIRCRAFT

"Enemy airmen appearing over our lines have been turned back or driven off by shell fire." - EXTRACT FROM DESPATCH.

Gardening is a hobby which does not exist under very favorable conditions at the front, its greatest drawback being that when the gardener's unit is moved from one place to another his garden cannot accompany him. Its devotees appear to derive a certain amount of satisfaction from the mere making of a garden, the laying-out and digging and planting; but it can be imagined that the most enthusiastic gardener would in time become discouraged by a long series of beginnings without any endings to his labors, to a frequent sowing and an entire absence of reaping.

There are, however, some units which, from the nature of their business, are stationary in one place for months on end, and here the gardener as a rule has an opportunity for the indulgence of his pursuit. In clearing-hospitals, ammu-nition-parks, and Army Service Corps supply points, there are, I believe, many such fixed abodes; but the manners and customs of the inhabitants of such happy resting-places are practically unknown to the men who live month in month out in a narrow territory, bounded on the east by the forward firing line and on the west by the line of the battery positions, or at farthest the villages of the reserve billets. In any case these places are rather outside the scope of tales dealing with what may be called the "Under Fire Front," and it was this front which I had in mind when I said that gardening did not receive much encouragement at the front. But during the first spring of the War I know of at least one enthusiast who did his utmost, metaphorically speaking, to beat his sword into a plowshare, and to turn aside at every opportunity from the duty of killing Germans to the pleasures of growing potatoes. He was a gunner in the detachment of the Blue Marines, which ran a couple of armored motor-cars carrying anti-aircraft guns.

It is one of the advantages of this branch of the air-war that when a suitable position is fixed on for defense of any other position, the detachment may stay there for some consi-derable time. There are other advantages which will unfold themselves to those initiated in the ways of the trench zone, although those outside of it may miss them; but everyone will see that prolonged stays in the one position give the gardener his opportunity. In this particular unit of the Blue Marines was a gunner who intensely loved the potting and planting, the turning over of yielding earth, the bedding-out and trans-planting, the watering and weeding and tending of a garden, possibly because the greater part of his life had been lived at sea in touch with nothing more yielding than a steel plate or a hard plank.

The gunner was known throughout the unit by no other name than Mary, fittingly taken from the nursery rhyme which inquires, "Mary, Mary, quite contrary, how does your garden grow?" The similarity between Mary of the Blue Marines and Mary of the nursery rhyme ends, however, with the first line, since Blue Marine Mary made no attempt to rear "silver bells and cockle shells" (whatever they may be) all in a row. His whole energies were devoted to the raising of much more practical things, like lettuces, radishes, carrots, spring onions, and any other vegetable which has the commendable reputation of arriving reasonably early at maturity.

Twice that spring Mary's labors had been wasted because the section had moved before the time was ripe from a gardener's point of view, and although Mary strove to transplant his garden by uprooting the vegetables, packing them away in a box in the motor, and planting them out in the new position, the vegetables failed to survive the breaking of their home ties, and languished and died in spite of Mary's tender care. After the first failure he tried to lay out a portable garden, enlisting the aid of "Chips" the carpenter in the manufacture of a number of boxes, in which he placed earth and his new seedlings. This attempt, however, failed even more disastrously than the first, the O.C. having made a most unpleasant fuss on the discovery of two large boxes of mustard and cress "cluttering up," as he called it, the gun-mountings on one of the armored cars, and, when the section moved suddenly in the dead of night, refusing point-blank to allow any available space to be loaded up with Mary's budding garden. Mary's plaintive inquiry as to what he was to do with the boxes was met by the brutal order to "chuck the lot overboard," and the counter-inquiry as to whether he thought this show was a perambulating botanical gardens.

So Mary lost his second garden complete, even unto the box of spring onions which were the apple of his gardening eye. But he brisked up when the new position was established and he learned through the officer's servant that the selected spot was considered an excellent one, and offered every prospect of being held by the section for a considerable time. He selected a favorable spot and proceeded once more to lay out a garden and to plant out a new lot of vegetables.

The section's new position was only some fifteen hundred yards from the forward trench; but, being at the bottom of a gently sloping ridge which ran between the position and the German lines, it was covered from all except air observation. The two armored cars, containing guns, were hidden away amongst the shattered ruins of a little hamlet; their armor-plated bodies, already rendered as inconspi-cuous as possible by erratic daubs of bright colors laid on after the most approved Futurist style, were further hidden by untidy wisps of straw, a few casual beams, and any other of the broken rubbish which had once been a village. The men had their quarters in the cellars of one of the broken houses, and the two officers inhabited the corner of a house with a more or less remaining roof.

Mary's garden was in a sunny corner of what had been in happier days the back garden of one of the cottages. The selection, as it turned out, was not altogether a happy one, because the garden, when abandoned by its former owner, had run to seed most liberally, and the whole of its area appeared to be impregnated with a variety of those seeds which give the most trouble to the new possessor of an old garden. Anyone with the real gardening instinct appears to have no difficulty in distinguishing between weeds and otherwise, even on their first appearance in shape of a microscopic green shoot; but flowers are not weeds, and Mary had a good deal of trouble to distinguish between the self-planted growths of nasturtiums, foxgloves, marigolds, forget-me-nots, and other flowers, and the more prosaic but useful carrots and spring onions which Mary had introduced. Probably a good many onions suffered the penalty of bad company, and were sacrificed in the belief that they were flowers; but on the whole the new garden did well, and began to show the trim rows of green shoots which afford such joy to the gardening soul. The shoots grew rapidly, and as time passed uneventfully and the section remained unmoved, the garden flourished and the vegetables drew near to the day when they would be fit for consumption.

Mary gloated over that garden; he went to a world of trouble with it, he bent over it and weeded it for hours on end; he watered it religiously every night, he even erected miniature forcing frames over some of the vegetable rows, ransacking the remains of the broken-down hamlet for squares of glass or for any pieces large enough for his purpose. He built these cunningly with frameworks of wood and untwisted strands of barbed wire, and there is no doubt they helped the growth of his garden immensely.

Although they have not been torched upon, it must not be supposed that Mary had no other duties. Despite our frequently announced "Supremacy of the Air," the anti-aircraft guns were in action rather frequently. The German aeroplanes in this part of the line appeared to ignore the repeated assurances in our Press that the German 'plane invariably makes off on the appearance of a British one; and although it is true that in almost every case the German was "turned back," he very frequently postponed the turning until he had sailed up and down the line a few times and seen, it may be supposed, all that there was to see.

At such times - and they happened as a rule at least once a day and occasionally two, three, or four times a day - Mary had to run from his gardening and help man the guns.

In the course of a month the section shot away many thousands of shells, and, it is to be hoped, severely frightened many German pilots, although at that time they could only claim to have brought down one 'plane, and that in a descent so far behind the German lines that its fate was uncertain.

It must be admitted that the gunners on the whole made excellent shooting, and if they did not destroy their target, or even make him turn back, they fulfilled the almost equally useful object of making him keep so high that he could do little useful observing. But the short periods of time spent by the section in shooting were no more than enough to add a pleasant flavor of sport to life, and on the whole, since the weather was good and the German gunnery was not - or at least not good enough to be troublesome to the section - life during that month moved very pleasantly.

But at last there came a day when it looked as if some of the inconveniences of war were due to arrive. The German aeroplane appeared as usual one morning just after the section had completed breakfast. The methodical regularity of hours kept by the German pilots added considerably to the comfort and convenience of the section by allowing them to time their hours of sleep, their meals, or an afternoon run by the O.C. on the motor into the near-by town, so as to fit in nicely with the duty of anti-aircraft guns.

On this morning at the usual hour the aeroplane appeared, and the gunners, who were waiting in handy proximity to the cars, jumped to their stations. The muzzles of the two-pounder pom-poms moved slowly after their target, and when the range-indicator told that it was within reach of their shells the first gun opened with a trial beltful. "Bang - bang - bang - bang!" it shouted, a string of shells singing and sighing on their way into silence. In a few seconds, "Puff - puff - puff - puff!" four pretty little white balls broke out and floated solid against the sky. They appeared well below their target, and both the muzzles tilted a little and barked off another flight of shells. This time they appeared to burst in beautiful proximity to the racing aeroplane, and immediately the two-pounders opened a steady and accurate bombardment. The shells were evidently dangerously close to the 'plane, for it tilted sharply and commenced to climb steadily; but it still held on its way over the British lines, and the course it was taking it was evident would bring it almost directly over the Blue Marines and their guns. The pom-poms continued their steady yap-yap, jerking and springing between each, round, like eager terriers jumping the length of their chain, recoiling and jumping, and yelping at every jump. But although the shells were dead in line the range was too great, and the guns slowed down their rate of fire, merely rapping off an occasional few rounds to keep the observer at a respectful distance, without an unnecessary waste of ammunition.

Arrived above them, the aeroplane banked steeply and swung round in a complete circle.

"Dash his impudence," growled the captain. "Slap at him again, just for luck." The only effect the resulting slap at him had, however, was to show the 'plane pilot that he was well out of range and to bring him spiraling steeply down a good thousand feet. This brought him within reach of the shells again, and both guns opened rapidly, dotting the sky thickly with beautiful white puffs of smoke, through which the enemy sailed swiftly. Then suddenly another shape and color of smoke appeared beneath him, and a red light burst from it flaring and floating slowly downwards. Another followed, and then another, and the 'plane straightened out its course, swerved, and flashed swiftly off down-wind, pursued to the limit of their range by the raving pom-poms. "Which it seems to me," said the Blue Marine sergeant reflectively, "that our Tauby had us spotted and was signaling his guns to call and leave a card on us."

That afternoon showed some proof of the correctness of the sergeant's supposition; a heavy shell soared over and dropped with a crash in an open field some two hundred yards beyond the outermost house of the hamlet. In five minutes another followed, and in the same field blew out a hole about twenty yards from the first. A third made another hole another twenty yards off, and a fourth again at the same interval.

When the performance ceased, the captain and his lieutenant held a conference over the matter. "It looks as if we'd have to shift," said the captain. "That fellow has got us marked down right enough."

"If he doesn't come any nearer," said the lieutenant, "we're all right. We won't need to take cover when the shelling starts, and even if the guns are shooting when the German is shelling, the armor-plate will easily stand off splinters from that distance."

"Yes," said the captain. "But do you suppose our friend the Flighty Hun won't have a peep at us to-morrow morning to see where those shells landed? If he does, or if he takes a photograph, those holes will show up like a chalk-mark on a blackboard; then he has only to tell his gun to step this way a couple of hundred yards and we get it in the neck. I'm inclined to think we'd better up anchor and away."

"We're pretty comfortable here, you know," urged the lieutenant, "and it's a pity to get out. It might be that those shots were blind chance. I vote for waiting another day, any-how, and seeing what happens. At the worst we can pack up and stand by with steam up; then if the shells pitch too near we can slip the cable and run for it"

"Right-oh!" said the captain.

Next morning the enemy aeroplane appeared again at its appointed hour and sailed overhead, leaving behind it a long wake of smoke-puffs; and at the same hour in the afternoon as the previous shelling the German gun opened fire, dropping its first shell neatly fifty yards further from the shell-holes of the day before. The aeroplane, of course, had reported, or its photograph had shown, the previous day's shells to have dropped apparently fifty yards to the left of the hamlet. The gun accordingly corrected its aim and opened fire on a spot fifty yards more to the right. For hours it bombarded that suffering field energetically, and at the end of that time, when they were satisfied the shelling was over, the Blue Marines climbed from their cellar. Next morning the aeroplane appeared again, and the Blue Marines allowed it this time to approach unattacked. Convinced probably by this and the appearance of the numerous shell-pits scattered round the gun position, the aeroplane swooped lower to verify its observations. Unfortunately another anti-aircraft gun a mile further along the line thought this too good an opportunity to miss, and opened rapid fire. The 'plane leaped upward and away, and the Blue Marines sped on its way with a stream of following shells.

"If the Huns' minds work on the fixed and appointed path, one would expect the same old field will get a strafing this afternoon," said the captain afterwards. "The airman will have seen the village knocked about, and if he knew that those last shells came from here he'll just conclude that yesterday's shooting missed us, and the gunners will have another whale at us this afternoon."

He was right; the gun had "another whale" at them, and again dug many holes in the old field.

But next morning the Germans played a new and disconcerting game. The aeroplane hovered high above and dropped a light, and a minute later the Blue Marines heard a shrill whistle, that grew and changed to a whoop, and ended with the same old crash in the same old field.

"Now," said the captain. "Stand by for trouble. That brute is spotting for his gun."

The aeroplane dropped a light, turned, and circled round to the left. Five minutes later another shell screamed over, and this time fell crashing into the hamlet. The hit was palpable and unmistakable; a huge dense cloud of smoke and mortar-, lime-, and red brick-dust leapt and billowed and hung heavily over the village.

"This," said the captain rapidly, "is where we do the rabbit act. Get to cover, all of you, and lie low."

They did the rabbit act, scuttling amongst the broken houses to the shelter of their cellar and diving hastily into it. Another shell arrived, shrieking wrathfully, smashed into another broken house, and scattered its ruins in a whirl-wind of flying fragments.

Now Mary, of course, was in the cellar with the rest, and Mary's garden was in full view from the cellar entrance, and twenty or twenty-five yards from it. The rest of the party were surprised to see Mary, as the loud clatter of falling stones subsided, leap for the cellar steps, run up them, and disappear out into the open. He was back in a couple of minutes. "I just wondered," he said breathlessly, "if those blighters had done any damage to my vegetables." When another shell came he popped up again for another look, and this time he dodged back and said many unprintable things until the next shell landed. He looked a little relieved when he came back this time. "This one was farther away," he said, "but that one afore dropped somebody's hearth-stone inside a dozen paces from my onion bed." For the next half-hour the big shells pounded the village, tearing the ruins apart, battering down the walls, blasting huge holes in the road and between the houses, re-destroying all that had already been destroyed, and completing the destruction of some of the few parts that had hitherto escaped.

Between rounds Mary ran up and looked out. Once he rushed across to his garden and came back cursing impo-tently, to report a shell fallen close to the garden, his carefully erected forcing frames shattered to splinters by the shock, and a hail of small stones and the ruins of an iron stove dropped obliteratingly across his carrots.

"If only they'd left this crazy shooting for another week," said Mary, "a whole lot of those things would have been ready for pulling up. The onions is pretty near big enough to eat now, and I've half a mind to pull some o' them before that cock-eyed Hun lands a shell in me garden and blows it to glory."

Later he ran out, pulled an onion, a carrot, and a lettuce, brought them back to the cellar, proudly passed them round, and anxiously demanded an opinion as to whether they were ready for pulling, and counsel as to whether he ought to strip his garden.

"Now look here!" said the sergeant at last; "you let your bloomin' garden alone; I'm not going to have you running out there plucking carrot and onion nosegays under fire. If a shell blows your garden half-way through to Australia, I can't help it, and neither can you. I'll be quite happy to split a dish of spuds with you if so be your garden offers them up; but I'm not going to have you casualtied rescuing your perishing radishes under fire. Nothing'll be said to me if your garden is strafed off the earth; but there's a whole lot going to be said if you are strafed along with it, and I have to report that you had disobeyed orders and not kept under cover, and that I had looked on while you broke ship and was blown to blazes with a boo-kay of onions in your hand. So just you anchor down there till the owner pipes to carry on."

Mary had no choice but to obey, and when at last the shelling was over he rushed to the garden and examined it with anxious care. He was in a more cheerful mood when he rejoined the others. "It ain't so bad," he said. "Total casualties, half the carrots killed, the radish-bed severely wounded (half a chimney-pot did that), and some o' the onions slightly wounded by bits of gravel. But what do you reckon the owner's going to do now? Has he given any orders yet?"

No orders had been given, but the betting amongst the Blue Marines was about ninety-seven to one in favor of their moving. Sure enough, orders were given to pack up and prepare to move as soon as it was dark, and the captain went off with a working party to reconnoiter a new position and prepare places for the cars. Mary was sent off in "the shore boat" (otherwise the light runabout which carried them on duty or pleasure to and from the ten-mile-distant town) with orders to draw the day's rations, collect the day's mail, buy the day's papers, and return to the village, being back not later than five o'clock.

It was made known that the position to which the captain contemplated moving was one in a clump of trees within half a mile of the position they were leaving. Mary was hugely satisfied. "That ain't half bad," he said when he heard. "I can walk over and water the garden at night, and pop across any time between the Tauby's usual promenade hours and do a bit o' weeding, and just keep an eye on things generally. And inside a week we're going to have carrots for dinner every day, *and* spring onions. Hey, my lads! what about bread and cheese and spring onions, wot?"

He climbed aboard the run-about, drove out of the yard, and rattled off down the road. He executed his commi-ssions, and was sailing happily back to the village, when about a mile short of it a sitting figure rose from the roadside, stepped forward, and waved an arresting hand. To his surprise, Mary saw that it was one of the Blue Marines.

"What's up?" he said, as the Marine came round to the side and proceeded to step on board.

"Orders," said the Marine briefly. "I was looking out for you. Change course and direction and steer for the new anchorage."

"The idea being wot!" asked Mary.

"We've been in action again," said the Marine gloomily. "Only two shells this time, but they did more damage than all the rest put together this morning."

"More damage?" gasped Mary. "Wot - wot have they damaged?"

The Marine ticked off the damages on his fingers one by one.

"Car hit, badly damaged, and down by the stern; gun out of action - mounting smashed; the sergeant hit, piece of his starboard leg carried away; and five men slightly wounded."

He dropped his hands, which Mary took as a sign that the tally was finished. "Is that all?" he said, and breathed a sigh of relief. "Strewth! I thought you was going to tell me that my garden had been gott-straffed."

A FRAGMENT

This is not a story, it is rather a fragment, beginning where usually a battle story ends, with a man being "casualtied," showing the principal character only in a passive part - a very passive part - and ending, I am afraid, with a lot of unsatisfactory loose ends ungathered up. I only tell it because I fancy that at the back of it you may find some hint of the spirit that has helped the British Army in many a tight corner.

Private Wally Ruthven was knocked out by the bursting of a couple of bombs in his battalion's charge on the front line German trenches. Any account of the charge need not be given here, except that it failed, and the battalion making it, or what was left of them, beaten back. Private Wally knew nothing of this, knew nothing of the renewed British bombardment, the renewed British attack half a dozen hours later, and again its renewed failure. All this time he was lying where the force of the bomb's explosion had thrown him, in a hole blasted out of the ground by a bursting shell. During all that time he was unconscious of anything except pain, although certainly he had enough of that to keep his mind very fully occupied. He was brought back to an agonizing consciousness by the hurried grip of strong hands and a wrenching lift that poured liquid flames of pain through every nerve in his mangled body. To say that he was badly wounded hardly describes the case; an R.A.M.C. orderly afterwards described his appearance with painful picturesqueness as "raw meat on a butcher's block," and indeed it is doubtful if the stretcher-bearers who lifted him from the shell-hole would not rather have left him lying there and given their brief time and badly needed services to a casualty more promising of recovery, if they had seen at first Private

Ruthven's serious condition. As it was, one stretcher-bearer thought and said the man was dead, and was for tipping him off the stretcher again. Ruthven heard that and opened his eyes to look at the speaker, although at the moment it would not have troubled him much if he had been tipped off again. But the other stretcher-bearer said there was still life in him; and partly because the ground about them was pattering with bullets, and the air about them clamant and reverberating with the rush and roar of passing and exploding shells and bombs, and that particular spot, therefore, no place or time for argument; partly because stretcher-bearers have a stubborn conviction and fundamental belief - which, by the way, has saved many a life even against their own momen-tary judgment - that while there is life there is hope, that a man "isn't dead till he's buried," and finally that a stretcher must always be brought in with a load, a live one if possible, and the nearest thing to alive if not, they brought him in.

The stretcher-bearers carried their burden into the front trench and there attempted to set about the first bandaging of their casualty. The job, however, was quite beyond them, but one of them succeeded in finding a doctor, who in all the uproar of a desperate battle was playing Mahomet to the mountain of such cases as could not come to him in the field dressing station. The orderly requested the doctor to come to the casualty, who was so badly wounded that "he near came to bits when we lifted him." The doctor, who had several urgent cases within arm's length of him as he worked at the moment, said that he would come as soon as he could, and told the orderly in the meantime to go and bandage any minor wounds his casualty might have. The bearer replied that there were no minor wounds, that the man was "just nothing but one big wound all over"; and as for bandaging, that he "might as well try to do first aid on a pound of meat that had run through a mincing machine." The doctor at last, hobbling painfully and leaning on the stretcher-bearer - for he himself had been twice wounded, once in the foot by a piece of shrapnel, and once through the tip of the shoulder by a rifle bullet - came to Private Ruthven. He spent a good deal of time and innumerable yards of bandages on him, so that when the stretcher-bearers brought him into the dressing station there was little but bandages to be seen of him. The stretcher-bearer delivered a message from the doctor that there was very little hope, so that Ruthven for the time being was merely given an injection of morphia and put aside.

The approaches to the dressing station and the station itself were under so severe a fire for some hours afterwards that it was impossible for any ambulance to be brought near it. Such casualties as could walk back walked, others were carried slowly and painfully to a point which the ambu-lances had a fair sporting chance of reaching intact. One way and another a good many hours passed before Ruthven's turn came to be removed. The doctor who had bandaged him in the firing-line had by then returned to the dressing station, mainly because his foot had become too painful to allow him to use it at all. Merely as an aside, and although it has nothing to do with Private Ruthven's case, it may be worth mentioning that the same doctor, having cleaned, sterilized, and bandaged his wounds, remained in the dressing station for another twelve hours, doing such work as could be accomplished sitting in a chair and with one sound and one unsound arm. He saw Private Ruthven for a moment as he was being started on his journey to the ambulance; he remembered the case, as indeed everyone who handled or saw that case remembered it for many days, and, moved by professional interest and some amazement that the man was still alive, he hobbled from his chair to look at him. He found Private Ruthven returning his look; for the passing of time and the excess of pain had by now overcome the effects of the morphia injection. There was a hauntingly appealing look in the eyes that looked up at him, and the doctor tried to answer the question he imagined those eyes would have conveyed.

"I don't know, my boy," he said, "whether you'll pull through, but we'll do the best we can for you. And now we have you here we'll have you back in hospital in no time, and there you'll get every chance there is."

He imagined the question remained in those eyes still unsatisfied, and that Ruthven gave just the suggestion of a slow head-shake.

"Don't give up, my boy," he said briskly. "We might save you yet. Now I'm going to take away the pain for you," and he called an orderly to bring a hypodermic injection. While he was finding a place among the bandages to make the injection, the orderly who was waiting spoke: "I believe, sir, he's trying to ask something or say something."

It has to be told here that Private Ruthven could say nothing in the terms of ordinary speech, and would never be able to do so again. Without going into details it will be enough to say that the whole lower part of - well, his face - was tightly bound about with bandages, leaving little more than his nostrils, part of his cheeks, and his eyes clear. He was frowning now and again, just shaking his head to denote a negative, and his left hand, bound to the bigness of a football in bandages, moved slowly in an endeavor to push aside the doctor's hands.

"It's all right, my lad," the doctor said soothingly. "I'm not going to hurt you."

The frown cleared for an instant and the eloquent eyes appeared to smile, as indeed the lad might well have smiled at the thought that anyone could "hurt" such a bundle of pain. But although it appeared quite evident that Ruthven did not want morphia, the doctor in his wisdom decreed otherwise, and the jolting journey down the rough shell-torn road, and the longer but smoother journey in the sweetly-sprung motor ambulance, were accomplished in sleep.

When he wakened again to consciousness he lay for some time looking about him, moving only his eyes and very slowly his head. He took in the canvas walls and roof of the big hospital marquee, the scarlet-blanketed beds, the flitting figures of a couple of silent-footed Sisters, the screens about two of the beds; the little clump of figures, doctor, orderlies, and Sister, stooped over another bed. Presently he caught the eye of a Sister as she passed swiftly the foot of his bed, and she, seeing the appealing look, the barely perceptible upward twitch of his head that was all he could do to beckon, stopped and turned, and moved quickly to his side. She smoothed the pillow about his head and the sheets across his shoulders, and spoke softly.

"I wonder if there is anything you want?" she said. "You can't tell me, can you? just close your eyes a minute if there is anything I can do. Shut them for yes - keep them open for no."

The eyes closed instantly, opened, and stared upward at her.

"Is it the pain?" she said. "Is it very dreadful?"

The eyes held steady and unflickering upon hers. She knew well that there they did not speak truth, and that the pain must indeed be very dreadful.

"We can stop the pain, you know," she said "Is that what you want?"

The steady unwinking eyes answered "No" again, and to add emphasis to it the bandaged head shook slowly from side to side on the pillow.

The Sister was puzzled; she could find out what he wanted, of course, she was confident of that; but it might take some time and many questions, and time just then was some-thing that she or no one else in the big clearing hospital could find enough of for the work in their hands. Even then urgent work was calling her; so she left him, promising to come again as soon as she could.

She spoke to the doctor, and presently he came back with her to the bedside. "It's marvelous," he said in a low tone to the Sister, "that he has held on to life so long."

Private Ruthven's wounds had been dressed there on arrival,

before he woke out of the morphia sleep, and the doctor had seen and knew.

"There is nothing we can do for him," he said, "except morphia again, to ease him out of his pain."

But again the boy, his brow wrinkling with the effort, attempted with his bandaged hand to stay the needle in the doctor's fingers.

"I'm sure," said the Sister, "he doesn't want the morphia; he told me so, didn't you?" appealing to the boy.

The eyes shut and gripped tight in an emphatic answer, and the Sister explained their code.

"Listen!" she said gently. "The doctor will only give you enough to make you sleep for two or three hours, and then I shall have time to come and talk to you. Will that do!"

The unmoving eyes answered "No" again, and the doctor stood up.

"If he can bear it, Sister," he said, "we may as well leave him. I can't understand it, though. I know how those wounds must hurt."

They left him then, and he lay for another couple of hours, his eyes set on the canvas roof above his head, dropped for an instant to any passing figure, lifting again to their fixed position. The eyes and the mute appeal in them haunted the Sister, and half a dozen times, as she moved about the beds, she flitted over to him, just to drop a word that she had not forgotten and she was coming presently.

"You want me to talk to you, don't you?" she said. "There is something you want me to find out?"

"Yes - yes - yes," said the quickly flickering eyelids.

The Sister read the label that was tied to him when he was brought in. She asked questions round the ward of those who were able to answer them, and sent an orderly to make inquiries in the other tents. He came back presently and reported the finding of another man who belonged to Ruthven's regiment and who knew him. So presently, when she was relieved from duty - the first relief for thirty-six solid hours of physical stress and heart-tearing strain - she went straight to the other tent and questioned the man who knew Private Ruthven. He had a hopelessly shattered arm, but appeared mightily content and amazingly cheerful. He knew Wally, he said, was in the same platoon with him; didn't know much about him except that he was a very decent sort; no, knew nothing about his people or his home, although he remembered - yes, there was a girl. Wally had shown him her photograph once, "and a real ripper she is too." Didn't know if Wally was engaged to her, or anything more about her, and certainly not her name.

The Sister went back to Wally. His wrinkled brow cleared at the sight of her, but she could see that the eyes were sunk more deeply in his head, that they were dulled, no doubt with his suffering.

"I'm going to ask you a lot of questions," she said, "and you'll just close your eyes again if I speak of what you want to tell me. You do want to tell me something, don't you?"

To her surprise, the "Yes" was not signaled back to her. She was puzzled a moment. "You want to ask me something?" she said.

"Yes," the eyelids flicked back.

"Is it about a girl?" she asked. ("No.")

"Is it about money of any sort?" ("No.")

"Is it about your mother, or your people, or your home? Is it about yourself?"

She had paused after each question and went on to the next, but seeing no sign of answering "Yes" she was baffled for a moment. But she felt that she could not go to her own bed to which she had been dismissed, could not go to the sleep she so badly needed, until she had found and answered the question in those pitiful eyes. She tried again.

"Is it about your regiment?" she asked, and the eyes snapped "Yes," and "Yes," and "Yes" again. She puzzled over that, and then went back to the doctor in charge of the other ward and brought back with her the man who "knew Wally." Mentally she clapped her hands at the light that leaped to the boy's eyes. She had told the man that it was something about the regiment he wanted to know; told him, too, his method of answering "Yes" and "No," and to put his questions in such, a form that they could be so answered.

The friend advanced to the bedside with clumsy caution.

"Hello, Wally!" he said cheerfully. "They've pretty well chewed you up and spit you out again, 'aven't they? But you're all right, old son, you're going to pull through, 'cause the O.C. o' the Linseed Lancers[Footnote: Medical Service.] here told me so. But Sister here tells me you want to ask something about someone in the old crush." He hesitated a moment. "I can't think who it would be," he confessed. "It can't be his own chum, 'cause he 'stopped one,' and Wally saw it and knew he was dead hours before. But look 'ere," he said determinedly, "I'll go through the whole bloomin' regiment, from the O.C. down to the cook, by name and one at a time, and you'll tip me a wink and stop me at the right one. I'll start off with our own platoon first; that ought to do it," he said to the Sister.

"Perhaps," she said quickly, "he wants to ask about one of his officers. Is that it?" And she turned to him.

The eyes looked at her long and steadily, and then closed

flutteringly and hesitatingly.

"We're coming near it," she said, "although he didn't seem sure about that 'Yes.'"

"Look 'ere," said the other, with a sudden inspiration, "there's no good o' this 'Yes' and 'No' guessin' game; Wally and me was both in the flag-wagging class, and we knows enough to - there you are." He broke off in triumph and nodded to Wally's flickering eyelids, that danced rapidly in the long and short of the Morse code.

"Y-e-s. Ac-ac-ac."[Footnote: Ac-ac-ac: three A's, denoting a full stop. In "Signalese" similar-sounding letters are given names to avoid confusion. A is Ac; T, Toe; D, Don; P, Pip; M, Emma, etc.]

"Yes," he said. "If you'll get a bit of paper, Sister, you can write down the message while I spells it off. That's what you want, ain't it, chum?"

The Sister took paper and pencil and wrote the letters one by one as the code ticked them off and the reader called them to her.

"Ready. Begins!" Go on, Miss, write it down," as she hesitated. "Don-I-Don - Did; W-E - we; Toc-ac-K-E - take; Toc-H-E - the; Toc-R-E-N-C-H - trench; ac-ac-ac. Did we take the trench?"

The signaler being a very unimaginative man, possibly it might never have occurred to him to lie, to have told anything but the blunt truth that they did not take the trench; that the regiment had been cut to pieces in the attempt to take it; that the further attempt of another regiment on the same trench had been beaten back with horrible loss; that the lines on both sides, when he was sent to the rear late at night, were held exactly as they had been held before the attack; that the whole result of the action was *nil* - except for the casualty list. But he caught just in time the softly sighing whispered "Yes" from the unmoving lips of the Sister, and he lied promptly and swiftly, efficiently and at full length.

"Yes," he said. "We took it. I thought you knew that, and that you was wounded the other side of it; we took it all right. Got a hammering of course, but what was left of us cleared it with the bayonet. You should 'ave 'eard 'em squeal when the bayonet took 'em. There was one big brute -"

He was proceeding with a cheerful imagination, colored by past experiences, when the Sister stopped him. Wally's eyes were closed.

"I think," she said quietly, "that's all that Wally wants to know. Isn't it, Wally?"

The lids lifted slowly and the Sister could have cried at the glory and satisfaction that shone in them. They closed once softly, lifted slowly, and closed again tiredly and gently. That is all. Wally died an hour afterwards.

AN OPEN TOWN

"Yesterday hostile artillery shelled the town of - some miles behind our lines, without military result. Several civilians were killed." - EXTRACT FROM DESPATCH.

Two officers were cashing checks in the Bank of France and chatting with the cashier, who was telling them about a bombardment of the town the day before. The bank had removed itself and its business to the underground vaults, and the large room on the ground floor, with its polished mahogany counters, brass grills and desks, loomed dim and indistinct in the light which filtered past the sandbags piled outside. The walls bore notices with a black hand pointing downwards to the cellar steps, and the big room echoed eerily to the footsteps of customers, who tramped across the tiled floor and disappeared downstairs to the vaults.

"One shell," the cashier was saying, "fell close outside there," waving a hand up the cellar steps. "*Bang! crash!* we feel the building shake - so." His hands left their task of counting notes, seized an imaginary person by the lapels of an imaginary coat and shook him violently.

"The noise, the great c-r-rash, the shoutings, the little squeals, and then the peoples running, the glasses breaking - tinkle - tinkle - you have seen the smoke, thick black smoke, and smelling - pah!"

He wrinkled his nose with disgust. "At first - for one second - I think the bank is hit; but no, it is the street outside. Little stones - yes, and splinters, through the windows; they come and hit all round, inside - rap, rap, rap!" His darting hand played the splinters' part, indicating with little pointing stabs the ceiling and the walls. "Mademoiselle there, you see? yes! one little piece of shell," and he held finger and thumb to illustrate an inch-long fragment.

The two officers looked at Mademoiselle, an exceedingly pretty young girl, sitting composedly at a typewriter. There was a strip of plaster marring the smooth cheek, and at the cashier's words she looked round at the young officers, flashed them a cheerful smile, and returned to her hammering on the keyboard.

"My word, Mademoiselle," said one of the officers. "Near thing, eh? I wonder you are not scared to carry on."

The girl turned a slightly puzzled glance on them.

"Monsieur means," explained the cashier friendlily to her, "is it that you have no fear - *peur*, to continue the affairs?"

Mademoiselle smiled brightly and shook her head. "But no," she said cheerfully, "it is nossings," and went back to her work.

"Jolly plucky girl, I think," said the officer. "Nearly as plucky as she is pretty. I say, old man, my French isn't up to handling a compliment like that; see if you can -"

He did not finish the sentence, for at that moment there was a faint far-off *bang*, and they sensed rather than felt a faint quiver in the solid earth beneath their feet. The cashier held up one hand and stood with head turned sideways in an attitude of listening.

"You hear?" he said, arching his eyebrows.

"What was it?" said the officer. "Sounded like a door banging upstairs."

"No, no," said the cashier. "They have commenced again. It is the same hour as last time, and the time before."

Mademoiselle had stopped typing, and the ledger clerk at the desk behind her had also ceased work and sat listening; but after a moment Mademoiselle threw a little smile towards them - a half-pleased, half-deprecating little smile, as of one who shows a visitor something interesting, something one is glad to show, and then resumed her clicking on the typewriter. The ledger clerk, too, went back to work, and the cashier said off-handedly: "It is not near - the station perhaps - yes!" as if the station were a few hundred miles off, instead of a few hundred yards. He finished rapidly counting his bundle of notes and handed them to the officer.

When the two emerged from the bank they found the street a good deal quieter than when they had entered it. They walked along towards the main square, noticing that some of the shopkeepers were calmly putting up their shutters, while others quietly continued serving the few customers who were hurriedly completing their purchases. As the two walked along the narrow street they heard the thin savage whistle of an approaching shell and a moment later a tremendous *bang*! They and everybody else near them stopped and looked round, up and down the street, and up over the roofs of the houses. They could see nothing, and had turned to walk on when something crashed sharply on a roof above them, bounced off, and fell with a rap on the cobble-stones in the street. A child, an eager-faced youngster, ran from an arched gateway and pounced on the little object, rose, and held up a piece of stone, with intense annoyance and disgust plainly written on his face, threw it from him with an exclamation of disappointment.

The two walked on chuckling. "Little bounder!" said one. "Thought he'd got a souvenir; rather a sell for him - what?"

In the main square, they found a number of market women packing up their little stalls and moving off, others debating volubly and looking up at the sky, pointing in the direction of the last sound, and clearly arguing with each other as to whether they should stay or move. A couple of Army Transport wagons clattered across the square. One driver, with the reins bunched up in his hand and the whip under his arm, was busily engaged striking matches and trying to light a cigarette; the other, allowing his horses to follow the first wagon, and with his mouth open, gazed up into the sky as if he expected to see the next shell coming. A few civilians scattered about the square were walking briskly; a woman, clutching the arm of a little boy, ran, dragging him, with his little legs going at a rapid trot. More civilians, a few men in khaki, and some in French uniform, were standing in archways or in shop-doors.

There was another long whistle, louder and harsher this time, and followed by a splintering crash and rattle. The groups in the doorways flicked out of sight; the people in the open half halted and turned to hurry on, or in some cases, without looking round, ran hurriedly to cover. Stones and little fragments of debris clacked down one by one, and then in a little pattering shower on the stones of the square. The last of the market women, hesitating no longer, hurriedly bundled up their belongings and hastened off. The two officers turned into a café with a wide front window, seated themselves near this at a little marble table, and ordered beer. There were about a score of officers in the room, talking or reading the English papers. All of them had very clean and very close-shaven faces, and very dirty and weather-stained, mud-marked clothes. For the most part they seemed a great deal more interested in each other, in their conversations, and in their papers, than in any notice of the bombardment. The two who were seated near the window had a good view from it, and extracted plenty of interest from watching the people outside.

Another shell whistled and roared down, burst with a deep angry bellow, a clattering and rending and splintering sound of breaking stone and wood. This time bigger fragments of stone, a shower of broken tiles and slates rattled down into the square; a thick cloud of dirty black smoke, gray and red tinged with mortar and brick-dust, appeared up above the roofs on the other side of the square, spread slowly and thickly, and hung long, dissolving very gradually and thinning off in trailing wisps.

In the cafe there was silence for a moment, and many remarks about "coming rather close" and "getting a bit unhealthy," and a jesting inquiry of the proprietor as to the shelter available in the cellar with the beer barrels. A few rose and moved over to the window; one or two opened the door, to stand there and look round.

"Look at that old girl in the doorway across there," said one. "You would think she was frightened she was going to get her best bonnet wet."

The woman's motions had, in fact, a curious resemblance to those of one who hesitated about venturing out in a heavy rainstorm. She stood in the doorway and looked round, drew back and spoke to someone inside, picked up a heavy basket, set it down, stepped into the door, glanced carefully and calculatingly up at the sky and across the square in the direction she meant to take, moved back again and picked up her basket, set it firmly on her arm, stepped out and comm- enced to hobble at an ungainly cumbersome trot across the square. She was no more than half-way across when the shriek of another shell was heard approaching. She stopped and cast a terrified glance about her, dumped the basket down on the cobbles, and resumed the shambling trot at increased speed. A soldier in khaki crossing the square also commenced to run for cover as his ear caught the sound of the shell; passing near the woman's basket, he stooped and grabbed it and doubled on with it after its panting owner.

A group of soldiers standing in the archway shouted laughter and encouragement, pretending they were watching a race, urging on the runners.

"Go on, Khaki! go on! - two to one on the fat girl; two to one -

I lay the fie-ald." Their cries and clapping shut off, and they disappeared like diving ducks as the shell roared down, struck with a horrible crash one of the buildings in a side-street just off the square, burst it open, and flung upward and outward a flash of blinding light, a spurt of smoke, a torrent of flying bricks and broken stones. Through the rattle and clatter of falling masonry and flying rubbish there came, piercing and shrill, the sound of a woman's screams. They choked off suddenly, and for some seconds there were no sounds but those of falling frag-ments, jarring and hailing on the cobble-stones, of broken glass crashing and tinkling from dozens of windows round the square.

As the noises of the explosion died away, figures crowded out anxiously into the doorways again, and stood there and about the pavements, looking round, pointing and gesticulating, and plainly prepared to run back under cover at the first sign of warning. The half-dozen men who had cheered the race across the square emerged from the archway, looked around, and then set off running, keeping close under the shelter of the houses, and disappearing into the thick smoke and dust that still hung a thick and writhing curtain about the street-end in the corner of the square.

The two officers who had sat at the cafe window looked at one another.

"You heard that squeal?" said one.

"Yes," said the other; "I think we might trot over. You knowing a little bit about surgery might be useful."

"Oh, I dunno," said the first. "But, anyhow, let's go."

They paid their bill and went out, and as they crossed the square they met a couple of the soldiers who had disappeared into the smoke. They were moving at the double, but at a word from the officers they halted. Both wore the Red Cross badge of the Army Medical Corps on their arms, and one explained hurriedly that they were going for an ambulance, that there was a woman killed, one man and a woman and two children badly wounded. They ran on, and the two officers moved hastily towards the shell-struck house. The smoke was clearing now, and it was possible to see something of the damage that had been done.

The shell apparently had struck the roof, had ripped and torn it off, burst downwards and outwards, blowing out the whole face of the upper story, the connecting-wall and corner of the houses next to it, part of the top-floor, and a jagged gap in the face of the lower story. The street was piled with broken bricks and tiles, with splinters of stone, with uprooted cobbles, with fragments and beams, bits of furniture, ragged-edged planks, fragments of smoldering cloth. As the two walked, their feet crunched on a layer of splintered glass and broken crockery. The air they breathed reeked with a sharp chemical odor and the stench of burning rags.

The R.A.M.C. men had collected the casualties, and were doing what they could for them, and the officer who was "a bit of a surgeon" gave them what help he could. The casualties were mangled cruelly, and one of them, a child, died before the ambulance came.

The shells began to come fast now. One after another they poured in, the last noise of their approach before they struck sounding like the rush and roar of an express train passing through a tunnel. No more fell near the square; but the two officers, returning across it, with the terrifying rush of its projectiles in their ears, moved hastily and puffed sighs of relief as they reached the door of the cafe again.

"I just about want a drink," said the one who was "a bit of a surgeon." "Thank Heaven I didn't decide to go into the Medical. The more I see of that job the less I like it."

The other shuddered. "How these surgeons do it at all," he said, "beats me. I had to go outside when you started to handle that kiddie. Sorry I couldn't stay to help you."

"It didn't matter," said the first. "Those Medical fellows did all I wanted, and anyhow you were better employed giving a hand to stop that building catching light."

The two had their drink and prepared to move again.

"Time we were off, I suppose," said the first. "Our lot must be getting ready to take the road presently, and we ought to be there."

So they moved and dodged through the quiet streets, with the shells still whooping overhead and bursting noisily in different parts of the town. On their way they entered a shop to buy some slabs of chocolate. The shop was empty when they entered, but a few stout raps on the counter brought a woman, pale-faced but volubly chattering, up a ladder and through a trapdoor in the shop-floor. She served them while the shells still moaned overhead, talking rapidly, apologizing for keeping them waiting, and explaining that for the children's sake she always went down into the cellar when the shelling commenced, wishing them, as they gathered up their parcels and left, "bonne chance," and making for the trap-door and the ladder as they closed the shop-door.

About the main streets there were few signs of the shells' work, except here and there a litter of fragments tossed over the roofs and sprayed across the road. But, passing through a small side square, the two officers saw something more of the effect of "direct hits." In the square was parked a number of ambulance wagons, and over a building at the side floated a huge Red Cross flag. Eight or nine shells had been dropped in and around the square. Where they had fallen were huge round holes, each with a scattered fringe of earth and cobble-stones and broken pavement. The trees lining the square showed big white patches on their trunks where the bark had been sliced by flying fragments, branches broken, hanging and dangling, or holding out jagged white stumps. Leaves and twigs and

BOYD CABLE

branches were littered about the square and heaped thick under the trees. The brick walls of many of the houses round were pitted and pocked and scarred by the shell fragments. The face of one house was marked by a huge splash, with solid center and a ragged-edged outline of radiating jerky rays, reminding one immediately of a famous ink-maker's advertisement. The bricks had taken the impression of the explosion's splash exactly as paper would take the ink's. Practically every window in the square had been broken, and in the case of the splash-marked house, blown in, sash and frame complete. One ambulance wagon lay a torn and splintered wreck, and pieces of it were flung wide to the four corners of the square. Another was overturned, with broken wheels collapsed under it, and in the Red Cross canvas tilts of others gaped huge tears and rents.

At one spot a pool of blood spread wide across the pavement, and still dripping and running sluggishly and thickly into and along the stone gutter, showed where at least one shell had caught more than brick and stone and tree, although now the square was deserted and empty of life.

And even as the two hurriedly skirted the place another shell hurtled over, tripped on the top edge of a roof across the square and exploded with an appalling clatter and burst of noise. The roof vanished in a whirlwind of smoke and dust, and the officers jumped from the doorway where they had flung themselves crouching, and finished their passage of the square at a run.

"Hottish corner," said one, as they slowed to a walk some distance away.

"Silly fools," growled the other. "What do they want to hoist that huge Red Cross flag up there for, where any airman can see it? Fairly asking for it, I call it."

When they came to the outskirts of the town they found rather more signs of life. People were hanging about their doorways and the shops, fewer windows were shuttered, fewer faces peeped from the tiny grated windows of the cellars. And up the center of the road, with lordly calm, marched three Highlanders. The smooth swing of their kilts, their even, unhurried step, the shoulders well back, and the elbows a shade outturned, the bonnets cocked to a precisely same angle on the upheld heads, all bespoke either an amazing ignorance of, or a bland indifference to, the bombardment. Their march was stopped by a sentry, who shouted to them and moved out from the pavement. Some sort of argument was going on as the officers approached, and in passing they heard the finish of it.

"You were pit there tae warn folk," a Highlander was saying. "Weel, ye've dune that, so we'll awa on oor road. We're nae fonder o' shells than y'are yersel. But we'd look bonnie, wouldn't we, t' be tellin' the Cameron lads we promised to meet, that we were feared for a bit shellin'...."

And after they had passed, the officers looked back and saw the three Scots swinging their kilts and swaggering imperturbably on to the town, and their meeting with the "Cameron lads."

There were no more shells, but that afternoon a Taube paid another of its frequent visits and vigorously bombed the railway station again, driving the inhabitants back once more to the inadequate shelter of their cellars and base-ments. And yet, as the same two officers marched with their battalion through the town towards the firing-line that evening, they found the streets quite normally bustling and astir, and there seemed to be no lack of light in the shops and houses and about the streets. Here and there as they passed, children stood stiffly to attention and gravely saluted the battalion, young women and old turned to call a cheery "Bonne Chance" to the soldiers, to smile bravely and wave farewells to them.

"Plucky bloomin' lot, ain't they, Bill?" said one man, and blew a kiss to three girls waving from a window.

"I takes off my 'at to them," said his mate. "What wi' Jack

Johnsons and airyplane bombs, you might expec' the population to have emigrated in a bunch. The Frenchmen is a plucky enough crowd, but the women - My Lord."

"Airyplanes every other day," said the first man. "But I don't notice any darkened streets and white-painted kerbs; and we don't 'ear the inhabitants shrieking about protection from air raids, or 'Where's the anti-aircraft guns?' or 'Who's responsible for air defense?' or 'A baa the Government that don't a baa the air raids!' 'say la gerr,' says they, and shrugs their shoulders, and leaves it go at that."

They were in a darker side-street now, and the glare of the burning house shone red in the sky over the roof tops. "Somebody's 'appy 'ome gone west," remarked one man, and a mouth-organ in the ranks answered, with cheerful sarcasm, "Keep the Home Fires Burning!"

THE SIGNALERS

"It is reported that ... " - EXTRACT FROM OFFICIAL DESPATCH.

The "it" and the "that" which were reported, and which the despatch related in another three or four lines, concerned the position of a forward line of battle, but have really nothing to do with this account, which aims only at relating something of the method by which "it was reported" and the men whose particular work was concerned only with the report as a report, a string of words, a jumble of letters, a huddle of Morse dots and dashes.

The Signaling Company in the forward lines was situated in a very damp and very cold cellar of a half-destroyed house. In it were two or three tables commandeered from upstairs or from some houses around. That one was a rough deal kitchen table, and that another was of polished wood, with beautiful inlaid work and artistic curved and carven legs, the spoils of some drawing-room apparently, was a matter without the faintest interest to the signalers who used them. To them a table was a table, no more and no less, a thing to hold a litter of papers, message forms, telephone gear, and a candle stuck in a bottle. If they had stopped to consider the matter, and had been asked, they would probably have given a dozen of the delicate inlaid tables for one of the rough strong kitchen ones. There were three or four chairs about the place, just as miscellaneous in their appearance as the tables. But beyond the tables and chairs there was no furniture whatever, unless a scanty heap of wet straw in one corner counts as furniture, which indeed it might well do since it counted as a bed.

There were fully a dozen men in the room, most of them orderlies for the carrying of messages to and from the telephonists. These men came and went continually. Outside it had been raining hard for the greater part of the day, and now, getting on towards midnight, the drizzle still held and the trenches and fields about the signalers' quarters were running wet, churned into a mass of gluey chalk-and-clay mud. The orderlies coming in with messages were daubed thick with the wet mud from boot-soles to shoulders, often with their puttees and knees and thighs dripping and running water as if they had just waded through a stream. Those who by the carrying of a message had just completed a turn of duty, reported themselves, handed over a message perhaps, slouched wearily over to the wall farthest from the door, dropped on the stone floor, bundled up a pack or a haversack, or anything else convenient for a pillow, lay down and spread a wet mackin-tosh over them, wriggled and composed their bodies into the most comfortable, or rather the least uncomfortable possible position, and in a few minutes were dead asleep.

It was nothing to them that every now and again the house above them shook and quivered to the shock of a heavy shell exploding somewhere on the ground round the house, that the rattle of rifle fire dwindled away at times to separate and scattered shots, brisked up again and rose to a long roll, the devil's tattoo of the machine guns rattling through it with exactly the sound a boy makes running a stick rapidly along a railing. The bursting shells and scourging rifle fire, sweeping machine guns, banging grenades and bombs were all affairs with which the Signaling Company in the cellar had no connection. For the time being the men in a row along the wall were as unconcerned in the progress of the battle as if they were safely and comfortably asleep in London. Presently any or all of them might be waked and sent out into the flying death and dangers of the battlefield, but in the meantime their immediate and only interest was in getting what sleep they could. Every once in a while the signalers' sergeant would shout for a man, go across to the line and rouse one of the sleepers; then the awakened man would sit up and blink, rise and listen to his instructions, nod and say, "Yes, Sergeant! All right, Sergeant!" when these were completed, pouch his message, hitch his damp mackintosh about him and button it close, drag heavily across the stone floor and vanish into the darkness of the stone-staired passage.

His journey might be a long or a short one, he might only have to find a company commander in the trenches one or two hundred yards away, he might on the other hand have a several hours' long trudge ahead of him, a bewildering way to pick through the darkness across a maze of fields and a net-work of trenches, over and between the rubble heaps that represented the remains of a village, along roads pitted with all sorts of blind traps in the way of shell holes, strings of barbed wire, overturned carts, broken branches of trees, flung stones and beams; and always, whether his journey was a short one or a long, he would move in an atmosphere of risk, with sudden death or searing pain passing him by at every step, and waiting for him, as he well knew, at the next step and the next and every other one to his journey's end.

Each man who took his instructions and pocketed his message and walked up the cellar steps knew that he might never walk down them again, that he might not take a dozen paces from them before the bullet found him. He knew that its finding might come in black dark and in the middle of an open field, that it might drop him there and leave him for the stretcher-bearers to find some time, or for the burying party to lift any time. Each man who carried out a message was aware that he might never deliver it, that when some other hand did so, and the message was being read, he might be past all messages, lying stark and cold in the mud and filth with the rain beating on his gray unheeding face; or, on the other hand, that he might be lying warm and comfortable in the soothing ease of a bed in the hospital train, swaying gently and lulled by the song of the flying wheels, the rock and roll of the long compartment, swinging at top speed down the line to the base and the hospital ship and home. An infinity of possibilities lay between the two extremes. They were undoubtedly the two extremes:

the death that each man hoped to evade, the wound whose painful prospect held no slightest terror but only rather the deep satisfaction of a task performed, of an escape from death at the cheap price of a few days' or weeks' pain, or even a crippled limb or a broken body.

A man forgot all these things when he came down the cellar steps and crept to a corner to snatch what sleep he could, but remembered them again only when he was wakened and sent out into their midst, and into all the toils and terrors the others had passed, or were to go into or even then were meeting.

The signalers at the instruments, the sergeants who gathered them in and sent them forth, gave little or no thought to the orderlies. These men were hardly more than shadows, things which brought them long screeds to be translated to the tapping keys, hands which would stretch into the candle-light and lift the messages that had just "buzzed" in over their wires. The sergeant thought of them mostly as a list of names to be ticked off one by one in a careful roster as each man did his turn of duty, went out, or came back and reported in. And the man who sent messages these men bore may never have given a thought to the hands that would carry them, unless perhaps to wonder vaguely whether the message could get through from so and so to such and such, from this map square to that, and if the chance of the messages getting through - the message you will note, not the messenger - seemed extra doubtful, orders might be given to send it in duplicate or triplicate, to double or treble the chances of its arriving.

The night wore on, the orderlies slept and woke, stumbled in and out; the telephonists droned out in monotonous voices to the telephone, or "buzzed" even more mono-tonous strings of longs and shorts on the "buzzer." And in the open about them, and all unheeded by them, men fought, and suffered wounds and died, or fought on in the scarce lesser suffering of cold and wet and hunger.

In the signalers' room all the fluctuations of the fight were translated from the pulsing fever, the human living tragedies and heroisms, the violent hopes and fears and anxieties of the battle line, to curt cold words, to scribbled letters on a message form. At times these messages were almost meaningless to them, or at least their red tragedy was unheeded. Their first thought when a message was handed in for transmission, usually their first question when the signaler at the other end called to take a message, was whether the message was a long one or a short one. One telephonist was handed an urgent message to send off, saying that bombs were running short in the forward line and that further supplies were required at the earliest possible moment, that the line was being severely bombed and unless they had the means to reply must be driven out or destroyed. The signaler took that message and sent it through; but his instrument was not working very clearly, and he was a good deal more concerned and his mind was much more fully taken up with the exasperating difficulty of making the signaler at the other end catch word or letter correctly, than it was with all the close packed volume of meaning it contained. It was not that he did not under-stand the meaning; he himself had known a line bombed out before now, the trenches rent and torn apart, the shattered limbs and broken bodies of the defenders, the horrible ripping crash of the bombs, the blinding flame, the numbing shock, the smoke and reek and noise of the explosions; but though all these things were known to him, the words "bombed out" meant no more now than nine letters of the alphabet and the maddening stupidity of the man at the other end, who would misunderstand the sound and meaning of "bombed" and had to have it in time-consuming letter-by-letter spelling.

When he had sent that message, he took off and wrote down one or two others from the signaling station he was in touch with. His own station, it will be remembered, was close up to the forward firing line, a new firing line which marked the limits of the advance made that morning. The station he was connected with was back in rear of what, previous to the attack, had been the British forward line. Between the two the thin insignificant thread of the telephone wire ran twisting across the jumble of the trenches of our old firing line, the neutral ground that had lain between the trenches, and the other maze of trench, dug-out, and bomb-proof shelter pits that had been captured from the enemy. Then in the middle of sending a message, the wire went dead, gave no answer to repeated calls on the "buzzer." The sergeant, called to consultation, helped to overlook and examine the instrument. Nothing could be found wrong with it, but to make quite sure the fault was not there, a spare instrument was coupled on to a short length of wire between it and the old one. They carried the message perfectly, so with curses of angry disgust the wire was pronounced disconnected, or "disc," as the signaler called it.

This meant that a man or men had to be sent out along the line to find and repair the break, and that until this was done, no telephone message could pass between that portion of the forward line and the headquarters in the rear. The situation was the more serious, inasmuch as this was the only connecting line for a considerable distance along the new front. A corporal and two men took a spare instrument and a coil of wire, and set out on their dangerous journey.

The break of course had been reported to the O.C., and after that there was nothing more for the signaler at the dead instrument to do, except to listen for the buzz that would come back from the repair party as they progressed along the line, tapping in occasionally to make sure that they still had connection with the forward station, their getting no reply at the same time from the rear station being of course sufficient proof that they had not passed the break.

Twice the signaler got a message, the second one being from the forward side of the old neutral ground in what had been the German front line trench; the report said also that fairly heavy fire was being maintained on the open ground. After that there was silence.

When the signaler had time to look about him, to light a

cigarette and to listen to the uproar of battle that filtered down the cellar steps and through the closed door, he spoke to the sergeant about the noise, and the sergeant agreed with him that it was getting louder, which meant either that the fight was getting hotter or coming closer. The answer to their doubts came swiftly to their hands in the shape of a note from the O.C., with a message borne by the orderly that it was to be sent through anyhow or somehow, but at once.

Now the O.C., be it noted, had already had a report that the telephone wire was cut; but he still scribbled his note, sent his message, and thereafter put the matter out of his mind. He did not know how or in what fashion the message would be sent; but he did know the Signaling Company, and that was sufficient for him.

In this he was doing nothing out of the usual. There are many commanders who do the same thing, and this, if you read it aright, is a compliment to the signaling companies beyond all the praise of General Orders or the sweet flattery of the G.O.C. despatch - the men who sent the messages put them out of their mind as soon as they were written and handed to an orderly with a curt order, "Signaling company to send that."

You at home who slip a letter into the pillar box, consider it, allowing due time for its journey, as good as delivered at the other end; by so doing you pay an unconscious compliment to all manners and grades of men, from high salaried managers down to humble porters and postmen. But the somewhat similar compliment that is paid by the men who send messages across the battlefield is paid in the bulk to one little select circle; to the animal brawn and blood, the spiritual courage and devotion, the bodies and brains, the pluck and perseverance, the endurance, the grit and the determination of the signaling companies.

When the sergeant took his message and glanced through it, he pursed his lips in a low whistle and asked the signaler to copy while he went and roused three messengers. His quick glance through the note had told him, even without the O.C.'s message, that it was to the last degree urgent that the message should go back and be delivered at once and without fail; therefore he sent three messengers, simply because three men trebled the chances of the message getting through without delay. If one man dropped, there were two to go on; if two fell, the third would still carry on; if he fell - well, after that the matter was beyond the sergeant's handling; he must leave it to the messenger to find another man or means to carry on the message.

The telephonist had scribbled a copy of the note to keep by him in case the wire was mended and the message could be sent through after the messengers started and before they reached the other end. The three received their instructions, drew their wet coats about their shivering shoulders, relieved their feelings in a few growled sentences about the dog's life a man led in that company, and departed into the wet night.

The sergeant came back, re-read the message and discussed it with the signaler. It said: "Heavy attack is developing and being pressed strongly on our center a-a-a.[Footnote: Three a's indicate a full stop.] Our losses have been heavy and line is considerably weakened a-a-a. Will hold on here to the last but urgently request that strong reinforcements be sent up if the line is to be maintained a-a-a. Additional artillery support would be useful a-a-a."

"Sounds healthy, don't it?" said the sergeant reflectively. The signaler nodded gloomily and listened apprehensively to the growing sounds of battle. Now that his mind was free from first thoughts of telephonic worries, he had time to consider outside matters. For nearly ten minutes the two men listened, and talked in short sentences, and listened again. The rattle of rifle fire was sustained and unbroken, and punctuated liberally at short intervals by the boom of exploding grenades and bombs. Decidedly the whole action was heavier - or coming back closer to them.

The sergeant was moving across the door to open it and listen when a shell struck the house above them. The building shook violently, down to the very flags of the stone floor; from overhead, after the first crash, there came a rumble of falling masonry, the splintering cracks of breaking wood-work, the clatter and rattle of cascading bricks and tiles. A shower of plaster grit fell from the cellar roof and settled thick upon the papers littered over the table. The sergeant halted abruptly with his hand on the cellar door, three or four of the sleepers stirred restlessly, one woke for a minute sufficiently to grumble curses and ask "what the blank was that"; the rest slept on serene and undisturbed. The sergeant stood there until the last sounds of falling rubbish had ceased. "A shell," he said, and drew a deep breath. "Plunk into upstairs somewhere."

The signaler made no answer. He was quite busy at the moment rearranging his disturbed papers and blowing the dust and grit off them.

A telephonist at another table commenced to take and write down a message. It came from the forward trench on the left, and merely said briefly that the attack on the center was spreading to them and that they were holding it with some difficulty. The message was sent up to the O.C. "Whoever the O.C. may be," as the sergeant said softly. "If the Colonel was upstairs when that shell hit, there's another O.C. now, most like." But the Colonel had escaped that shell and sent a message back to the left trench to hang on, and that he had asked for reenforcements.

"He did ask," said the sergeant grimly, "but when he's going to get 'em is a different pair o' shoes. It'll take those messengers most of an hour to get there, even if they dodge all the lead on the way."

As the minutes passed, it became more and more plain that the need for reenforcements was growing more and more urgent. The sergeant was standing now at the open door of the cellar, and the noise of the conflict swept down and clamored and beat about them.

"Think I'll just slip up and have a look round," said the sergeant. "I shan't be long."

When he had gone, the signaler rose and closed the door; it was cold enough, as he very sensibly argued, and his being able to hear the fighting better would do nothing to affect its issue. Just after came another call on his instrument, and the repair party told him they had crossed the neutral ground, had one man wounded in the arm, that he was going on with them, and they were still following up the wire. The message ceased, and the telephonist, leaning his elbows on the table and his chin on his hands, was almost asleep before he realized it. He wakened with a jerk, lit another cigarette, and stamped up and down the room trying to warm his numbed feet.

First one orderly and then another brought in messages to be sent to the other trenches, and the signaler held them a minute and gathered some more particulars as to how the fight was progressing up there. The particulars were not encouraging. We must have lost a lot of men, since the whole place was clotted up with casualties that kept coming in quicker than the stretcher-bearers could move them. The rifle-fire was hot, the bombing was still hotter, and the shelling was perhaps the hottest and most horrible of all. Of the last the signaler hardly required an account; the growling thumps of heavy shells exploding, kept sending little shivers down the cellar walls, the shiver being, oddly enough, more emphatic when the wail of the falling shell ended in a muffled thump that proclaimed the missile "blind" or "a dud." Another hurried messenger plunged down the steps with a note written by the adjutant to say the colonel was severely wounded and had sent for the second in command to take over. Ten more dragging minutes passed, and now the separate little shivers and thrills that shook the cellar walls had merged and run together. The rolling crash of the falling shells and the bursting of bombs came close and fast one upon another, and at intervals the terrific detonation of an aerial torpedo dwarfed for the moment all the other sounds.

By now the noise was so great that even the sleepers began to stir, and one or two of them to wake. One sat up and asked the telephonist, sitting idle over his instrument, what was happening. He was told briefly, and told also that the line was "disc." He expressed considerable annoyance at this, grumbling that he knew what it meant - more trips in the mud and under fire to take the messages the wire should have carried.

"Do you think there's any chance of them pushing in the line and rushing this house?" he asked. The telephonist didn't know. "Well," said the man and lay down again. "It's none o' my dashed business if they do anyway. I only hope we're tipped the wink in time to shunt out o' here; I've no particular fancy for sitting in a cellar with the Boche cock-shying their bombs down the steps at me." Then he shut his eyes and went to sleep again.

The morsed key signal for his own company buzzed rapidly on the signaler's telephone and he caught the voice of the corporal who had taken out the repair party. They had found the break, the corporal said, and were mending it. He should be through - he was through - could he hear the other end? The signaler could hear the other end calling him and he promptly tapped off the answering signal and spoke into his instrument. He could hear the morse signals on the buzzer plain enough, but the voice was faint and indistinct. The signaler caught the corporal before he withdrew his tap-in and implored him to search along and find the leakage.

"It's bad enough," he said, "to get all these messages through by voice. I haven't a dog's chance of doing it if I have to buzz each one."

The rear station spoke again and informed him that he had several urgent messages waiting. The forward signaler replied that he also had several messages, and one in particular was urgent above all others.

"The blanky line is being pushed in," he said. "No, it isn't pushed in yet - I didn't say it - I said being pushed in - being - being, looks like it will be pushed in - got that? The O.C. has' stopped one' and the second has taken command. This message I want you to take is shrieking for reenforcements - what? I can't hear - no I didn't say anything about horses - I did *not*. Reenforcements I said; anyhow, take this message and get it through quick."

He was interrupted by another terrific crash, a fresh and louder outburst of the din outside; running footsteps clattered and leaped down the stairs, the door flung open and the sergeant rushed in slamming the door violently behind him. He ran straight across to the recumbent figures and began violently to shake and kick them into wakefulness.

"Up with ye!" he said, "every man. If you don't wake quick now, you'll maybe not have the chance to wake at all."

The men rolled over and sat and stood up blinking stupidly at him and listening in amazement to the noise outside.

"Rouse yourselves," he cried. "Get a move on. The Germans are almost on top of us. The front line's falling back. They'll stand here." He seized one or two of them and pushed them towards the door. "You," he said, "and you and you, get outside and round the back there. See if you can get a pickaxe, a trenching tool, anything, and break down that grating and knock a bigger hole in the window. We may have to crawl out there presently. The rest o' ye come with me an' help block up the door."

Through the din that followed, the telephonist fought to get his message through; he had to give up an attempt to speak it while a hatchet, a crowbar, and a pickaxe were noisily at work breaking out a fresh exit from the back of the cellar, and even after that work had been completed, it was difficult to make himself heard. He completed the urgent message for reenforcements at last, listened to some confused and confusing comments upon it, and then made ready to take some messages from the other end.

"You'll have to shout," he said, "no, shout - speak loud, because I can't 'ardly 'ear myself think - no, 'ear myself think. Oh, all sorts, but the shelling is the worst, and one o' them beastly airyale torpedoes. All right, go ahead."

The earpiece receiver strapped tightly over one ear, left his right hand free to use a pencil, and as he took the spoken message word by word, he wrote it on the pad of message forms under his hand. Under the circumstances it is hardly surprising that the message took a good deal longer than a normal time to send through, and while he was taking it, the signaler's mind was altogether too occupied to pay any attention to the progress of events above and around him. But now the sergeant came back and warned him that he had better get his things ready and put together as far as he could, in case they had to make a quick and sudden move.

"The game's up, I'm afraid," he said gloomily, and took a note that was brought down by another orderly. "I thought so," he commented, as he read it hastily and passed it to the other signaler. "It's a message warning the right and left flanks that we can't hold the center any longer, and that they are to commence falling back to conform to our retirement at 3.20 *ac emma*, which is ten minutes from now."

Over their heads the signalers could hear tramping scurrying feet, the hammering out of loopholes, the dragging thump and flinging down of obstacles piled up as an additional defense to the rickety walls. Then there were more hurrying footsteps, and presently the jarring *rap-rap-rap* of a machine gun immediately over their heads.

"That's done it!" said the sergeant. "We've got no orders to move, but I'm going to chance it and establish an alter-native signaling station in one of the trenches somewhere behind here. This cellar roof is too thin to stop an ordinary Fizzbang, much less a good solid Crump, and that machine gun upstairs is a certain invitation to sudden death and the German gunners to down and out us."

He moved towards the new opening that had been made in the wall of the cellar, scrambled up it and disappeared. All the signalers lifted their attention from their instruments at the same moment and sat listening to the fresh note that ran through the renewed and louder clamor and racket. The signaler who was in touch with the rear station called them and began to tell them what was happening.

"We're about all in, I b'lieve," he said. "Five minutes ago we passed word to the flanks to fall back in ten minutes. What? Yes, it's thick. I don't know how many men we've lost hanging on, and I suppose we'll lose as many again taking back the trench we're to give up. What's that? No. I don't see how reenforcements could be here yet. How long ago you say you passed orders for them to move up? An hour ago! That's wrong, because the messengers can't have been back - telephone message? That's a lot less than an hour ago. I sent it myself no more than half an hour since. Oo-oo! did you get that bump? Dunno, couple o' big shells or something dropped just outside. I can 'ardly 'ear you. There's a most almighty row going on all round. They must be charging, I think, or our front line's fallen back, because the rifles is going nineteen to the dozen, a-a-ah! They're getting stronger too, and it sounds like a lot more bombs going; hold on, there's that blighting maxim again."

He stopped speaking while upstairs the maxim clattered off belt after belt of cartridges. The other signalers were shuffling their feet anxiously and looking about them.

"Are we going to stick it here?" said one. "Didn't the sergeant say something about 'opping it?"

"If he did," said the other, "he hasn't given any orders that I've heard. I suppose he'll come back and do that, and we've just got to carry on till then."

The men had to shout now to make themselves heard to each other above the constant clatter of the maxim and the roar of rifle fire. By now they could hear, too, shouts and cries and the trampling rush of many footsteps. The signaler spoke into his instrument again.

"I think the line's fallen back," he said. "I can hear a heap o' men running about there outside, and now I suppose us here is about due to get it in the neck."

There was a scuffle, a rush, and a plunge, and the sergeant shot down through the rear opening and out into the cellar.

"The flank trenches!" he shouted. "Quick! Get on to them - right and left flank - tell them they're to stand fast. Quick, now, give them that first. Stand fast; do not retire."

The signalers leaped to their instruments, buzzed off the call, and getting through, rattled their messages off.

"Ask them," said the sergeant anxiously. "Had they commenced to retire." He breathed a sigh of relief when the answers came. "No," that the message had just stopped them in time.

"Then," he said, "you can go ahead now and tell them the order to retire is cancelled, that the reenforcements have arrived, that they're up in our forward line, and we can hold it good - oh!"

He paused and wiped his wet forehead; "you," he said, turning to the other signaler, "tell them behind there the same thing."

"How in thunder did they manage it, sergeant?" said the perplexed signaler. "They haven't had time since they got my message through."

"No," said the sergeant, "but they've just had time since they got mine."

"Got yours?" said the bewildered signaler.

"Yes, didn't I tell you?" said the sergeant. "When I went out for a look round that time, I found an artillery signaler laying out a new line, and I got him to let me tap in and send a message through his battery to headquarters."

"You might have told me," said the aggrieved signaler. "It would have saved me a heap of sweat getting that message through." After he had finished his message to the rear station he spoke reflectively: "Lucky thing you did get through," he said. "'Twas a pretty close shave. The O.C. should have a 'thank you' for you over it."

"I don't suppose," answered the sergeant, "the O.C. will ever know or ever trouble about it; he sent a message to the signaling company to send through - and it was sent through. There's the beginning and the end of it."

And as he said, so it was; or rather the end of it was in those three words that appeared later in the despatch: "It is reported."

CONSCRIPT COURAGE

You must know plenty of people - if you yourself are not one of them - who hold out stoutly against any military compulsion or conscription in the belief that the "fetched" man can never be the equal in valor and fighting instinct of the volunteer, can only be a source of weakness in any platoon, company and regiment. This tale may throw a new light on that argument.

Gerald Bunthrop was not a conscript in the strict sense of the word, because when he enlisted no legal form of conscription existed in the United Kingdom; but he was, as many more have been, a moral conscript, a man utterly averse to any form of soldiering, much less fighting, very reluctantly driven into the Army by force of circumstance and pressure from without himself. Before the War the Army and its ways were to him a sealed book. Of war he had the haziest ideas compounded of novels he had read and dimly remembered and mental pictures in a confused jumble of Charles O'Malley dragoons on spirited charges, half-forgotten illustrations in the papers of pith-helmeted infantry in the Boer War, faint boyhood recollections of Magersfontein and the glumness of the "Black Week" - a much more realistic and vivid impression of Waterloo as described by Brigadier Gerard - and odd figures of black Soudanese, of Light Brigade troopers, of Peninsula red-coats, of Sepoys and bonneted Highlanders in the Mutiny period, and of Life Guard sentries at Whitehall, lines of fixed bayonets on City procession routes, and khaki-clad Terriers seen about railway stations and on bus-tops with incongruous rifles on Saturday afternoons. Actually, it is not correct to include these living figures in his vague idea of war. They had to him no connection with anything outside normal peaceful life, stirred his thoughts to war no more than seeing a gasbracket would wake him to imaginings of a coalmine or a pit explosion. His slight conceptions of war, then, were a mere matter of print and books and pictures, and the first months of this present war were exactly the same, no more and no less - newspaper paragraphs and photos and drawings in the weeklies hanging on the bookstalls. He read about the Retreat and the Advance, skimmed the prophets' forecasts, gulped the communiques with interest a good deal fainter than he read the accounts of the football matches or a boxing bout. He expected "our side" to win of course, and was quite patriotic; was in fact a "supporter" of the British Army in exactly the sense of being a "supporter" or "follower" of Tottenham Hotspurs or Kent County. Any thoughts that he might shoulder a rifle and fight Germans would at that time, if it had entered his head, have seemed just as ridiculous as a thought that he should play in the Final at the Crystal Palace or step into the ring to fight Carpentier. It took a long time to move him from this attitude of aloofness. Recruiting posters failed utterly to touch him. He looked at them, criticized them, even discussed their "goodness" or drawing power on recruits with complete detachment and without the vaguest idea that they were addressed to him. He bought Allies' flag-buttons, and subscribed with his fellow-employees to a Red Cross Fund, and joined them again in sending some sixpences to a newspaper Smokes Gift Fund; he always most scrupulously stood up and uncovered to "God Save the King," and clapped and encored vociferously any patriotic songs or sentiments from the stage. He thought he was doing his full duty as a loyal Briton, and even - this was when he promised a regular sixpence a week to the Smokes Fund - going perhaps a little beyond it. First hints and suggestions that he should enlist he treated as an excellent jest, and when at last they became too frequent and pointed for that, and began to come from complete strangers, he became justly indignant at such "impudence" and "interference," and began long explainings to people he knew, that he wasn't the one to be bullied into anything, that fighting wasn't "his line," that he "had no liking for soldiering," that he would have gone like a shot, but had his own good and adequate reasons for not doing so.

There is no need to tell of the stages by which he arrived at the conclusion that he must enlist: from the first dawning wonder at such a possibility, through qualms of doubt and fear and spasms of hope and - almost - courage, to a dull apathy of resignation. No need to tell either the particular circumstances that "conscripted" him at last, because although his name is not real the man himself is, and one has no wish to bring shame on him or his people. I have only described him so closely to make it very clear that he was driven to enlistment, that a less promising recruit never joined up, that he was a conscript in every real sense of the word. We can pass over all his training, his introduction to the life of the trenches, his feelings of terror under conditions as little dangerous as the trenches could be. He managed, more or less, to hide this terror, as many a worse and many a better man has done before him, until one day -

The Germans had made a fierce attack, had overborne a section of the defense and taken a good deal of trenched ground, had been counter-attacked and partly driven back, had scourged the lost parts with a fresh tempest of artillery fire and driven in again to close quarters, to hot bomb and bayonet work; were again checked and for the moment held.

Private Gerald Bunthrop's battalion had been hurried up to support the broken and breaking line, was thrust into a badly wrecked trench with crumbling sides and broken traverses, with many dead and wounded cumbering the feet of the few defenders, with a reek of high-explosive fumes catching their throats and nostrils. The open ground beyond the trench was scattered thick with great heaps of German dead, a few more sprawled on the broken parapet, another and lesser few were huddled in the trench itself amongst the many khaki forms. The battalion holding the trench had been almost annihilated in the task, had in fact at first been driven out from part of the line and had only reoccupied it with heavy losses. Bunthrop

had with his battalion passed along some smashed communication trenches and over the open ground this fighting had
covered, and the sights they saw in passing might easily have
shaken the stoutest hearts and nerves. They made the
approach, too, under a destructive fire with high-explosive
shells screaming and crashing over, around, and amongst
them, with bullets whistling and hissing about them and
striking the ground with the sound of constantly exploding
Chinese crackers.

Bunthrop himself, to state the fact baldly, was in an agony of
fear. He might have been tempted to bolt, but was restrained
by a complete lack of any idea where to bolt to, by a lingering
remnant of self-respect, and by a firm conviction that he
would be dealt with mercilessly if he openly ran. But when he
reached the comparative shelter of the broken trench all these
safeguards of his decent behavior vanished. He flung himself
into the trench, cowered in its deepest part, made not the
slightest attempt to look over the parapet, much less to use his
rifle. There is this much of excuse for him, that on the very
instant that they reached the cover of the trench a bursting
high-explosive had caught the four men next in line to him.
The excuse may be insufficient for those who have never
witnessed at very close hand the instant and terrible destruction of four companions with whom they have eaten and slept
and talked and moved and had their intimate being for many
months; but those who have known such happenings will
understand. Bunthrop's sergeant understood, and because he
was a good sergeant and had the instinct for the right handling
of men - it must have been an instinct, because, up to a year
before, he had been ledger clerk in a City office and had
handled nothing more alive than columns of figures in a book
- he issued exactly the order that appealed exactly to
Bunthrop's terror and roused him from a shivering
embodiment of fear to a live thinking and order-obeying
private. "Get up and sling some of those sandbags back on the
parapet, Bunthrop!" he said, "and see if you can't make some
decent cover for yourself. You've nothing there that would
stop a half-crippled Hun jumping in on top of you." When he

came back along the trench five minutes later he found Bunthrop feverishly busy re-piling sandbags and strengthening the parapet, ducking hastily and crouching low when a shell roared past overhead, but hurriedly resuming work the instant it had passed. Then came the fresh German attack, preceded by five minutes' intense artillery fire, concentrated on the half-wrecked trench. The inferno of noise, the rush and roar of the approaching shells, the crash and earth-shaking thunder of their explosions, the ear-splitting cracks overhead of high-explosive shrapnel, the drone and whirr and thump of their flying fragments - the whole racking, roaring, deafening, sense-destroying tempest of noise was too much for Bunthrop's nerve. He flung down and flattened himself to the trench bottom again, squeezing himself close to the earth, submerged and drowned in a sweeping wave of panic fear. He gave no heed to the orders of his platoon commander, the shouting of his sergeant, the stir that ran along the trench, the flat spitting reports of the rifles that began to crack rapidly in a swiftly increasing volume of fire. A huge fragment of shell came down and struck the trench bottom with a suggestively violent thud a foot from his head. Half sick with the instant thought, "If it had been a foot this way!..." half crazed with the sense of openness to such a missile, Bunthrop rose to his knees, pressing close to the forward parapet, and looking wildly about him. His sergeant saw him. "You, Bunthrop," he shouted, "are you hit? Get up, you fool, and shoot! If we can't stop 'em before they reach here we're done in." Bunthrop hardly heeded him. Along the trench the men were shooting at top speed over the parapet; a dozen paces away two of the battalion machine-guns were clattering and racketing in rapid gusts of fire; a little farther along a third one had jambed and was being jerked and hammered at by a couple of sweating men and a wildly cursing boy officer. So much Bunthrop saw, and then with a hideous screeching roar a high explosive fell and burst in a shattering crash, a spouting hurricane of noise and smoke and flung earth and fragments. Bunthrop found himself half buried in a landslide of crumbling trench, struggled desperately clear, gasping and choking in the black cloud of smoke and fumes, saw presently, as the smoke thinned and dissolved, a chaos of broken earth and sandbags where the machine-guns had stood; saw one man and an officer dragging their gun from the debris, setting it up again on the broken edge of the trench. Another man staggered up the crumbling earth bank to help, and presently amongst them they got the gun into action again. The officer left it and ran to where he saw the other gun half buried in loose earth. He dragged it clear, found it undamaged, looked round, shouted at Bunthrop crouching flat against the trench wall; shouted again, came down the earth bank to him with a rush. "Come and help!" he yelled, grabbing at Bunthrop's arm. Bunthrop mumbled stupidly in reply. "What?" shouted the officer. "Come and help, will you? Never mind if you are hurt," as he noticed a smear of blood on the private's face. "You'll be hurt worse if they get into this trench with the bayonet. Come on and help!" Bunthrop, hardly understanding, obeyed the stronger will and followed him back to the gun. "Can you load?" demanded the officer. "Can you fill the cartridges into these drums while I shoot?" Bunthrop had had in a remote period of his training some machine-gun instruction. He nodded and mumbled again. "God!" said the officer. "Look at 'em! There's enough to eat us if they get to bayonet distance! We *must* stop 'em with the bullet. Hurry up, man; hurry, if you don't want to be skewered like a stuck pig!" He rattled off burst after burst of fire, clamoring at Bunthrop to hurry, hurry, hurry. A wounded machine-gunner joined them, and then some others, and the gun began to spit a steady string of bullets again. By this time the full meaning of the officer's words - the meaning, too, of remarks between the wounded helpers - had soaked into Bunthrop's brain. Their only hope, his only hope of life, lay in stopping the attack before it reached the trench; and the machine-guns were a main factor in the stopping. He lost interest in everything except cramming the cartridges into their place. When the officer was hit and rolled backwards and lay groaning and swearing, Bunthrop's chief and agonizing thought was that they - he - had lost the assistance and protection of the gun. When one of the wounded gunners took the officer's place and reopened fire, Bunthrop's only concern again was to keep pace with the loading. The thoughts were repeated exactly when that gunner was hit and collapsed and his place was taken by another man. And by now the urgent need of keeping the gun going was so impressed on Bunthrop that when the next gunner was struck down and the gun stood idle and deserted it was Bunthrop who turned wildly urging the other loaders to get up and keep the gun going; babbled excitedly about the only hope being to stop the Germans before they "got in" with the bayonet, repeated again and again at them the officer's phrase about "skewered like stuck pigs." The others hung back. They had seen man after man struck down at the gun, they could hear the *hiss* and *whitt* of the bullets over their heads, the constant cracker-like smacks of others that hit the parapet, and - they hung back. "Why th' 'ell don't you do it yerself?" demanded one of them, angered by Bunthrop's goading and in some degree, no doubt, by the disagreeable knowledge that they were flinching from a duty.

And then Bunthrop, the "conscript," the man who had held back from war to the last possible minute, who hated soldiering and shrank from violence and all fighting, who was known to his fellows as "a funk," the source of much uneasiness to company and platoon commanders and sergeants as "a weak spot," Bunthrop did what these others, these average good men who had "joined up" freely, who had longed for the end of home training and the transfer "out Front," dared not do. Bunthrop scrambled up the broken bank, seized the gun, swung the sights full to the broad gray target, and opened fire. He kept it going steadily, too, with a sleet of bullets whistling and whipping past him, kept on after a bullet snatched the cap from his head, and others in quick succession cut away a shoulder strap, scored a red weal across his neck, stabbed through the point of his shoulder. And when a shell-fragment smashed the gun under his hands, he left it only to plunge hastily to the other gun abandoned by all but dead and dying; pulled off a dead man who sprawled across it and recommenced shooting. He stopped firing only when his last cartridge was gone; squatted a moment longer staring over the sights, and then raised his head and peered out into the trailing film of smoke clouds from the bursting shells. Although it took him a minute to be sure of it he saw plainly at last that the attack was broken. Dimly he could see the heaped clusters of dead that lay out in the open, the crawling and limping figures of the wounded who sought safety back in the cover of their own trench, and more than that he could see men running with their heads stooped and their gray coats flapping about their ankles. It was this last that roused him again to action. He scrambled hurriedly back down the broken parapet into the trench. "Come on, you fellows," he shouted to two or three nearby men who continued to fire their rifles over the parapet. "It's no use waitin' here any longer." A heavy shell whooped roaring over them and crashed thunderously close behind the parapet. Bunthrop paid no slightest heed to it. His wide, staring eyes and white face, and blood smeared from the trickling wound in his neck, his capless head and tumbled hair, his clay and mud-caked and blood-stained uniform all gave him a look of wildness, of desperation, of abandonment. His sergeant, the man who had seen his fear and set him to pile the sandbags, caught sight of him again now, heard some word of his shoutings, and pushed hastily along the trench to where he fidgeted and called angrily to the others to "chuck that silly shooting - I'm goin' anyhow ... what's the use...."

The sergeant interrupted sharply.

"Here, you shut up, Bunthrop," he shouted. "Keep down in the trench. You're wounded, aren't you? Well, you'll get back presently."

"That be damn," said Bunthrop. "You don't understand. They're runnin' away, but we can't go out after 'em if these silly blighters here keep shootin'. Come on now, or they'll all be gone." And Private Bunthrop, the despised "conscript," slung his bayoneted rifle over his wounded shoulder and commenced to scramble up out over the front of the broken parapet. And what is more he was really and genuinely annoyed when the sergeant catching him by the heel dragged him down again and ordered him to stay there.

"Don't you understand?" he stuttered excitedly, and gesticulating fiercely towards the front. "They're runnin', I tell you; the blighters are runnin' away. Why can't we get out after 'em?"

SMASHING THE COUNTER-ATTACK

" ... *a violent counter-attack was delivered but was successfully repulsed at every point with heavy losses to the enemy.*" - EXTRACT FROM OFFICIAL DESPATCH.

There appears to be some doubt as to who rightly claims to have been the first to notice and report signs of the massing of heavy forces of Germans for the counter-attack on our positions. The infantry say that a scouting patrol fumbling about in the darkness in front of the forward fire trench heard suspicious sounds - little clickings of equipment and accouterments, stealthy rustlings, distant tramping - and reported on their return to the trench. An artillery observing officer is said to have seen flitting shadows of figures in the gray light of the dawn mists, and, later, an odd glimpse of cautious movement amongst the trees of a wood some little distance behind the German lines, and an unbroken passing of gray-covered heads behind a portion of a communication trench parapet. He also reported, and he may have been responsible for the dozen or so of shrapnel that were flung tentatively into and over the wood. An airman droning high over the lines, with fleecy white puffs of shrapnel smoke breaking about him, also saw and reported clearly "large force of Germans massing Map Square So-and-so."

But whoever was responsible for the first report matters little. The great point is that the movement was detected in good time, apparently before the preparations for attack were complete, so that the final arraying and disposal of the force for the launching of the attack was hampered and checked, and made perforce under a demoralizing artillery fire.

What the results might have been if the full weight of the massed attack could have been prepared without detection and flung on our lines without warning is hard to say; but there is every chance that our first line at least might have been broken into and swamped by the sheer weight of numbers. That, clearly, is what the Germans had intended, and from the number of men employed it is evident that they meant to push to the full any chance our breaking line gave them to reoccupy and hold fast a considerable portion of the ground they had lost. It is said that three to four full divisions were used. If that is correct, it is certain that the German army was minus three to four effective divisions when the attack withdrew, that a good half of the men in them would never fight again. The attack lost its first great advantage in losing the element of surprise. The bulk of the troops would have been moved into position in the hours of darkness. That wood, in all probability, was filled with men by night. The only daylight movement attempted would have been the cautious filling of the trenches, the pouring in of the long gray-coated lines along the communication trenches, all keeping well down and under cover. Under the elaborate system of deep trenches, fire-, and support-, communication- and approach-trenches running back for miles to emerge only behind houses or hill or wood, it is surprising how large a mass of men can be pushed into the forward trenches without any disclosure of movement to the enemy. Scores of thousands of men may be packed away waiting motionless for the word, more thousands may be pouring slowly up the communication ways, and still more thousands standing ready a mile or two behind the lines; and yet to any eye looking from the enemy's side the country is empty and still, and bare of life as a swept barn. Even the all-seeing airmen can be cheated, and see nothing but the usual quiet countryside, the tangled crisscross of trenches, looking from above like so many wriggling lines of thin white braid with a black cord-center, the neat dolls' toy-houses and streets of the villages, the straight, broad ribbon of the Route Nationale, all still and lifeless, except for an odd cart or two on the high road, a few dotted figures in the village streets. Below the flying-men the packed thousands are crouched still to

BOYD CABLE

earth. At the sound of the engine's drone, at sight of the wheeling shape, square miles of country stiffen to immobility, men scurry under cover of wall or bush, the long, moving lines in the trenches halt and sink down and hang their heads (next to movement the light dots of upturned, staring faces are the quickest and surest betrayal of the earth-men to the air-men), the open roads are emptied of men into the ditches and under the trees. For civilized man, in his latest art of war, has gone back to be taught one more simple lesson by the beasts of the field and birds of the air; the armed hosts are hushed and stilled by the passing air-machine, exactly as the finches and field-mice of hedgerow and ditch and field are frozen to stillness by the shadow of a hovering hawk, the beat of its passing wing.

But this time some movement in the trenches, some delay in halting a regiment, some neglect to keep men under cover, some transport too suspiciously close-spaced on the roads, betrayed the movement. His suspicions aroused, the airman would have risked the anti-aircraft guns and dropped a few hundred feet and narrowly searched each hillside and wood for the telltale gray against the green. Then the wireless would commence to talk, or the 'plane swoop round and drive headlong for home to report.

And then, picture the bustle at the different headquarters, the stir amongst the signalers, the frantic pipings of the telephone "buzzers," the sharp calls. "Take a message. Ready? Brigade H.Q. to O.C. Such-and-such Battery," or "to O.C. So-and-So Regiment"; imagine the furtive scurry in the trenches to man the parapets, and prepare bombs, and lay out more ammunition; the rush at the batteries, the quick consulting of squared maps, the bellowed string of orders in a jargon of angles of sight, correctors, ranges, figures and measures of degrees and yards, the first scramble about the guns dropping to the smooth work of ordered movement, the peering gun muzzles jerking and twitching to their ordained angles, the click and slam of the closing breech-blocks, the tense stillness as each gun reports "Ready!" and waits the word to fire.

And all the while imagine the Germans out there, creeping through the trees, crowding along the trenches, sifting out and settling down into the old favorite formation, making all ready for one more desperate trial of it, stacking the cards for yet another deep gambling plunge on the great German game - the massed attack in solid lines at close interval. The plan no doubt was the same old plan - a quick and overwhelming torrent of shell fire, a sudden hurricane of high explosive on the forward trench, and then, before the supports could be hurried up and brought in any weight through the reeking, shaking inferno of the shell-smitten communication trenches, the surge forward of line upon line, wave upon wave, of close-locked infantry.

But the density of mass, the solid breadth, the depth, bulk, and weight of men so irresistible at close-quarter work, is an invitation to utter destruction if it is caught by the guns before it can move. And so this time it was caught. Given their target, given the word "Go," the guns wasted no moment. The first battery ready burst a quick couple of ranging shots over the wood. A spray of torn leaves whirling from the tree tops, the toss of a broken branch, showed the range correct; and before the first rounds' solid white cotton-wooly balls of smoke had thinned and disappeared, puff-puff-puff the shrapnel commenced to burst in clouds over the wood. That was the beginning. Gun after gun, battery after battery, picked up the range and poured shells over and into the wood, went searching every hollow and hole, rending and destroying trench and dug-out, parapet and parados. The trenches, clean white streaks and zig-zags of chalk on a green slope, made perfect targets on which the guns made perfect shooting; the wood was a mark that no gun could miss, and surely no gun missed. What the scene in that wood must have been is beyond imagining and beyond telling. It was quickly shrouded in a pall of drifting smoke, and dimly through this the observing officers directing the fire of their guns could see clouds of leaves and twigs whirling and leaping under the lashing shrapnel, could see branches and smashed tree-trunks and great clods of earth and stone flying upward and outward from the blast of the lyddite shells. The wood was slashed to ribbons, rent and riddled to tatters, deluged from above with tearing blizzards of shrapnel bullets, scorched and riven with high-explosive shells. In the trenches our men cowered at first, listening in awe to the rushing whirlwinds of the shells' passage over their heads, the roar of the cannonade behind them, the crash and boom of the bursting shells in front, the shriek and whirr of flying splinters, the splintering crash of the shattering trees.

The German artillery strove to pick up the plan of the attack, to beat down the torrent of our batteries' fire, to smash in the forward trenches, shake the defense, open the way for the massed attack. But the contest was too unequal, the devastation amongst the crowded mass of German infantry too awful to be allowed to continue. Plainly the attack, ready or not ready, had to be launched at speed, or perish where it stood.

And so it was that our New Armies had a glimpse of what the old "Contemptible Little Army" has seen and faced so often, the huge gray bulk looming through the drifting smoke, the packed mass of the old German infantry attack. There were some of these "Old Contemptibles," as they proudly style themselves now, who said when it was all over, and they had time to think of anything but loading and firing a red-hot rifle, that this attack did not compare favorably with the German attacks of the Mons-Marne days, that it lacked something of the steadiness, the rolling majesty of power, the swinging stride of the old attacks; that it did not come so far or so fast, that beaten back it took longer to rally and come again, that coming again it was easier than ever to bring to a stand. But against that these "Old Contemptibles" admit that they never in the old days fought under such favorable conditions, that here in this fight they were in better constructed and deeper trenches, that they were far better provided with machine-guns, and, above all, that they had never, never, never had such a magnificent backing from our guns, such a tremen-dous stream of shells helping to smash the attack.

And smashed, hopelessly and horribly smashed, the attack assuredly was. The woods in and behind which the German hordes were massed lay from three to four hundred yards from the muzzles of our rifles. Imagine it, you men who were not there, you men of the New Armies still training at home, you riflemen practicing and striving to work up the number of aimed rounds fired in "the mad minute," you machine-gunners riddling holes in a target or a row of posts. Imagine it, oh you Artillery, imagine the target lavishly displayed in solid blocks in the open, with a good four hundred yards of ground to go under your streaming gun-muzzles. The gunners who were there that day will tell you how they used that target, will tell you how they stretched themselves to the call for "gun-fire" (which is an order for each gun to act independently, to fire and keep on firing as fast as it can be served), how the guns grew hotter and hotter, till the paint bubbled and blistered and flaked off them in patches, till the breech burned the incautious hand laid on it, till spurts of oil had to be sluiced into the breech from a can between rounds and sizzled and boiled like fat in a frying-pan as it fell on the hot steel, how the whole gun smoked and reeked with heated oil, and how the gun-detachments were half-deaf for days after.

It was such a target as gunners in their fondest dreams dare hardly hope for; and such a target as war may never see again, for surely the fate of such massed attacks will be a warning to all infantry commanders for all time.

The guns took their toll, and where death from above missed, death from the level came in an unbroken torrent of bullets sleeting across the open from rifles and machine-guns. On our trenches shells were still bursting, maxim and rifle bullets were still pelting from somewhere in half enfilade at long range. But our men had no time to pay heed to these. They hitched themselves well up on the parapet to get the fuller view of their mark; their officers for the most part had no need to bother about directing or controlling the fire - what need, indeed, to direct with such a target bulking big before the sights? What need to control when the only speed limit was a man's capacity to aim and fire? So the officers, for the most part, took rifle themselves and helped pelt lead into the slaughter-pit.

There are few, if any, who can give details of how or when the attack perished. A thick haze of smoke from the bursting shells blurred the picture. To the eyes of the defenders there was only a picture of that smoke-fog, with a gray wall of men looming through it, moving, walking, running towards them, falling and rolling, and looming up again and coming on, melting away into tangled heaps that disappeared again behind advancing men, who in turn became more falling and fallen piles. It was like watching those chariot races in a theater where the horses gallop on a stage revolving under their feet, and for all their fury of motion always remain in the same place. So it was with the German line - it was pressing furiously forward, but always appeared to remain stationary or to advance so slowly that it gave no impression of advancing, but merely of growing bigger. Once, or perhaps twice, the advancing line disappeared altogether, melted away behind the drifting smoke, leaving only the mass of dark blotches sprawled on the grass. At these times the fire died away along a part of our front, and the men paused to gulp a drink from a water-bottle, to look round and tilt their caps back and wipe the sweat from their brows, to gasp joyful remarks to one another about "gettin' a bit of our own back," and "this pays for the ninth o' May," and then listen to the full, deep roar of rifle-fire that rolled out from further down the line, and try to peer through the shifting smoke to see how "the lot next door" was faring. But these respites were short. A call and a crackle of fire at their elbows brought them back to business, to the grim business of purposeful and methodical killing, of wiping out that moving wall that was coming steadily at them again through the smoke and flame of the bursting shells. The great bulk of the line came no nearer than a hundred yards from our line; part pressed in another twenty or thirty yards, and odd bunches of the dead were found still closer. But none came to grips - none, indeed, were found within forty yards of our rifles' wall of fire. A scattered remnant of the attackers ran back, some whole and some hurt, thousands crawled away wounded, to reach the safe shelter of their support trenches, some to be struck down by the shells that still kept pounding down upon the death-swept field. The counter-attack was smashed - hopelessly and horribly smashed.

A GENERAL ACTION

"At some points our lines have been slightly advanced and their position improved." - EXTRACT FROM DESPATCH

It has to be admitted by all who know him that the average British soldier has a deep-rooted and emphatic objection to "fatigues," all trench-digging and pick-and-shovel work being included under that title. This applies to the New Armies as well as the Old, and when one remembers the safety conferred by a good deep trench and the fact that few men are anxious to be killed sooner than is strictly necessary, the objection is regrettable and very surprising. Still there it is, and any officer will tell you that his men look on trench-digging with distaste, have to be constantly persuaded and chivvied into doing anything like their best at it, and on the whole would apparently much rather take their chance in a shallow or poorly-constructed trench than be at the labor of making it deep and safe.

But one piece of trench-digging performed by the Tearaway Rifles must come pretty near a record for speed.

When the Rifles moved in for their regular spell in the forward line, their O.C. was instructed that his battalion had to construct a section of new trench in ground in front of the forward trench.

It was particularly unfortunate that just about this time the winter issue of a regular rum ration had ceased, and that, immediately before they moved in, a number of the Tearaways had been put under stoppages of pay for an escapade with which this story need have no concern.

Without pay the men, of course, were cut off from even the sour and watery delights of the beer sold in the local estaminets, which abound in the villages where the troops are billeted in reserve some miles behind the firing line. As Sergeant Clancy feelingly remarked:

"They stopped the pay, and that stops the beer; and then they stopped the rum. It's no pleasure in life they leave us at all, at all. They'll be afther stopping the fighting next."

Of that last, however, there was comparatively little fear at the moment. A brisk action had opened some days before the Tearaways were brought up from the reserve, and the forward line which they were now sent in to occupy had been a German trench less than a week before.

The main fighting had died down, but because the British were suspicious of counter-attacks, and the Germans afraid of a continued British movement, the opposing lines were very fully on the alert; the artillery on both sides were indulging in constant dueling, and the infantry were doing everything possible to prevent any sudden advantage being snatched by the other side.

As soon as the Tearaways were established in the new position, the O.C. and the adjutant made a tour of their lines, carefully reconnoitering through their periscopes the open ground which had been pointed out to them on the map as the line of the new trench which they were to commence digging. At this point the forward trench was curved sharply inward, and the new trench was designed to run across and outwards from the ends of the curve, meeting in a wide angle at a point where a hole had been dug and a listening-post established.

It was only possible to reach this listening-post by night, and the half-dozen men in it had to remain there throughout the day, since it was impossible to move across the open between the post and the trenches by daylight. The right-hand portion of the new trench running from the listening-post back to the forward trench had already been sketched out with entrenching tools, but it formed no cover because it was enfiladed by a portion of the German trench.

It was the day when the Tearaways moved into the new position, and the O.C. had been instructed that he was expected to commence digging operations as soon as it was dark that night, the method and manner of digging being left entirely in his own hand. The Major, the Adjutant, and a couple of Captains conferred gloomily over the prospec-tive task. That reputation of a dislike for digging stood in the way of a quick job being made. The stoppage of the rum ration prevented even an inducement in the shape of an "extra tot" being promised for extra good work, and it was well known to all the officers that the stoppage of pay had put the men in a sulky humor, which made them a little hard to handle, and harder to drive than the proverbial pigs. It was decided that nothing should be said to the men of the task ahead of them until it was time to tell off the fatigue party and start them on the work.

"It's no good," said the Captain, "leaving them all the afternoon to chew it over. They'd only be talking them-selves into a state that is first cousin to insubordination."

"I wish," said the other Captain, "they had asked us to go across and take another slice of the German trench. The men would do it a lot quicker and surer, and a lot more willing, than they'd dig a new one."

"The men," said the Colonel tartly, "are not going to be asked what they'd like any more than I've been. I want you each to go down quietly and have a look over at the new ground, tell the company commanders what the job is, and have a talk with me after as to what you think is the best way of setting about it."

That afternoon Lieutenant Riley and Lieutenant Brock took turns in peering through a periscope at the line of the new trench, and discussed the problem presented.

"It's all very fine," grumbled Riley, "for the O.C. to say the men must dig because he says so. You can take a horse to the water where you can't make it drink, and by the same token you can put a spade in a man's hand where you can't make him dig, or if he does dig he'll only do it as slow and gingerly as if it were his own grave and he was to be buried in it as soon as it was ready."

"Don't talk about burying," retorted Brock. "It isn't a pleasant subject with so many candidates for a funeral scattered around the front door."

He sniffed the air, and made an exclamation of disgust:

"They haven't even been chloride-of-limed," he said. "A lot of lazy, untidy brutes that battalion must have been we have just relieved."

Riley stared again into the periscope: "It's German the most of them are, anyway," he said, "that's one consolation, although it's small comfort to a sense of smell. I say, have a look at that man lying over there, out to the left of the listening-post. His head is towards us, and his hair is white as driven snow. They must be getting hard up for men to be using up the grandfathers of that age."

Brock examined the white head carefully. "He's a pretty old stager," he said, "unless he's a young 'un whose hair has turned white in a night like they do in novels; or, maybe he's a General."

"A General!" said Riley, and stopped abruptly. "Man, now, wait a minute. A General!" he continued musingly, and then suddenly burst into chuckles, and nudged Brock in the ribs. "I have a great notion," he said, "gr-r-reat notion, Brockie.

What'll you bet I don't get the men coming to us before night with a petition to be allowed to do some digging?"

Brock stared at him. "You're out of your senses," he said. "I'd as soon expect them to come with a petition to be allowed to sign the pledge."

"Well, now listen," said Riley, "and we'll try it, anyway."

He explained swiftly, while over Brock's face a gentle smile beamed and widened into subdued chucklings.

"Here's Sergeant Clancy coming along the trench," said Riley. "You have the notion now, so play up to me, and make sure Clancy hears every word you say."

"I want to see that General of theirs the Bosche prisoner spoke about," said Riley, as Clancy came well within earshot. "An old man, the Bosche said he was, with a head of hair as white and shining as a gull's wing."

"I'm not so interested in his shining head," said Brock, "as I am in the shining gold he carries on him. Doesn't it seem sinful waste for all that good money to be lying out there?"

Out of the tail of his eye Riley saw the sergeant halt and stiffen into an attitude of listening. He turned round.

"Was it me you wanted to see, Clancy?" he said.

"No, sorr - yes, sorr," said Clancy hurriedly, and then more slowly, in neat adoption of the remarks he had just heard: "Leastways, sorr, I was just afther wondering if you had heard anything of this tale of a German Gineral lying out there on the ground beyanst."

"You mean the one that was shot last week?" said Riley.

"Him with the five thousand francs in his breeches pocket, and the diamond-studded gold watch on his wrist?" said Brock.

"The same, sorr, the same!" said Clancy eagerly, and with his eyes glistening. "And have you made out which of them he is, sorr?"

"No," said Riley shortly. "And remember, Sergeant, there are to be no men going over the parapet this night without orders. The last battalion in here lost a big handful of men trying to get hold of that General, but the Germans were watching too close, and they've got a machine-gun trained to cover him. See to it, Clancy! That's all now."

Sergeant Clancy moved off, but he went reluctantly.

"Why didn't you give him a bit more?" asked Brock.

"Because I know Clancy," said Riley, whispering. "If we had said more now, he might have suspected a plant. As it is, he's got enough to tickle his curiosity, and you can be sure it won't be long before a gentle pumping performance is in operation."

Sergeant Clancy came in sight round the traverse again, moving briskly, but obviously slowing down as he passed them, and very obviously straining to hear anything they were saying. But they both kept silent, and when he had disappeared round the next traverse, Riley grinned and winked at his companion.

"He's hooked, Brockie," he said exultantly.

"Now you wait and - " He stopped as a rifle-man moved round the corner and took up a position on the firing step near them.

"I'll bet," said Riley delightedly, "Clancy has put him there to listen to anything he can catch us saying."

He turned to the man, who was clipping a tiny mirror on to

his bayonet and hoisting it to use as a periscope.

"Are you on the look-out?" he asked. "And who posted you there?"

"It was Sergeant Clancy, sir," answered the man. "He said I could hear better - I mean, see better," he corrected himself, "from here."

Riley abruptly turned to their own periscope and apparently resumed the conversation.

"I'm almost sure that's him with the white head," said Riley. "Out there, about forty or fifty yards from the German parapet, and about a hundred yards ten o'clock from our listening-post. Have a look."

He handed the periscope over to Brock, and at the same time noticed how eagerly the sentry was also having a look into his own periscope.

"I've got him," said Brock. "Yes, I believe that's the man."

"What makes it more certain," said Riley, "is that hen's scratch of a trench the other battalion started to dig out to the listening-post. They couldn't crawl out in the open to get to the General, and it's my belief they meant to drive a sap out to the listening-post, and then out to the General, and yank him in, so they could go through his pockets."

"It's a good bit of work to get at a dead man," said Brock reflectively.

"It is," said Riley, "but it isn't often you can drive a sap with five thousand francs at the end of it."

"To say nothing of a diamond-studded gold watch," said Brock.

"Well, well," said Riley, "I suppose the Germans won't be leaving him lying out there much longer. I hear the last battalion bagged quite a bunch that tried to creep out at night to get him in; but I suppose our fellows, not knowing about it, won't watch him so carefully."

They turned the conversation to other and more casual things, and shortly afterwards moved off.

The first-fruits of their sowing showed within the hour, when some of the officers were having tea together in a corner of a ruined cottage, which had been converted into a keep.

The servant who was preparing tea had placed a battered pot on the half of a broken door, which served for a mess table; had laid out a loaf of bread, tin pots of jam, a cake, and a flattened box of flattened chocolates, and these offices having been fully performed he should have retired. Instead, however, he fidgeted to and fro, offered to pour the tea from the dented coffee-pot, asked if anything more was wanted, pushed the loaf over to the Captain, apologizing at length for the impossibility of getting a scrape of butter these days; hovered round the table, and generally made it plain that he had something he wished to say, or that he supposed they had something to say he wished to hear.

"What are you dodging about there for, man?" the Captain asked irritably at last. "Is it anything you want?"

"Nothing, sorr," said the man, "only I was just wondering if you had heard annything of a Gineral with fifty thousand francs in his pocket, lying out there beyond the trench."

"Five thousand francs," corrected Riley gently.

"'Twas fifty thousand I heard, sorr," said the man eagerly; "but ye have heard, then, sorr?"

"What's this about a General?" demanded the Captain.

"Yes!" said Riley quickly. "What is it? We have heard nothing of the General."

"Ah!" said the messman, eyeing him thoughtfully, "I thought maybe ye had heard."

"We have heard nothing," said Riley. "What is it you are talking about?"

"About them fifty thousand francs, sorr," said the messman, cunningly, "or five thousand, was it?"

"What's this?" said the Captain, and the others making no attempt to answer his question, left the messman to tell a voluble tale of a German General ("though 'twas a Field-Marshal some said it was, and others went the length of Von Kluck himself") who had been killed some days before, and lay out in the open with five thousand, or fifty thousand, francs in his breeches pocket, a diamond-studded gold watch on his wrist, diamond rings on his fingers, and his breast covered with Iron Crosses and jeweled Orders.

That both Riley and Brock, as well as the Captain, professed their profound ignorance of the tale only served, as they well knew, to strengthen the Tearaways Rifles' belief in it, and after the man had gone they imparted their plan with huge delight and joyful anticipation to the Captain.

When they had finished tea and left the keep to return to their own posts, they were met by Sergeant Clancy.

"I just wanted to speak wid you a moment, sorr," he said. "I have been looking at that listening-post, and thinking to myself wouldn't it be as well if we ran a sap out to it; it would save the crawling out across the open at night, and keeping the men - and some wounded among them maybe - cooped up the whole day."

"There's something in that," said the Captain, pretending to reflect. "And I see the last battalion had made something of a beginning to dig a trench out to the post."

"And they must have been thinking with their boots when they dug it there," said Riley. "A trench on that side is open to enfilade fire. It should have been dug out from the left corner of that curve instead of the right."

"If you would speak to the O.C. about it, sorr," said Clancy, "he might be willing to let us dig it. The men is fresh, too, and won't harm for a bit of exercise."

"Very well," said the Captain carelessly, "we'll see about it to-morrow."

"Begging your pardon, sorr," said Clancy, "I was thinking it would be a good night tonight, seein' there's a strong wind blowing that would deaden the sound of the digging."

"That's true enough," the Captain said slowly. "I think it's an excellent idea, Clancy, and I'll speak to the O.C., and tell him you suggested it."

A few minutes after, an orderly brought a message that the O.C. was coming round the trenches to see the company commanders. The company commanders found him with rather a sharp edge to his temper, and Captain Conroy, to whom Riley and Brock had confided the secret of their plans, concluded the moment was not a happy one for explaining the ruse to the O.C. He, therefore, merely took his instructions for the detailing of a working party from his company, and the hour at which they were to commence.

"And remember," said the O.C. sharply, "you will stand no nonsense over this work. If you think any man is loafing or not doing his full share, make him a prisoner, or do anything else you think fit. I'll back you in it, whatever it is."

Conroy murmured a "Very good, sir," and left it at that. When he returned to his company he made arrangements for the working party, implying subtly to Sergeant Clancy that the trench was to be started as the result of his, the sergeant's, arguments.

Clancy went back to the men in high feather:

"I suppose now," he said complacently, "there's some would be like to laugh if they were told that a blessed sergeant could be saying where and when he'd be having this trench or that trench dug or not dug; but there's more ways of killing a cat than choking it with butter, and Ould Prickles can take a hint as good as the next man when it's put to him right."

"Prickles," be it noted, being the fitting, if somewhat disrespectful, name which the O.C. carried in the Rifles.

"It's yourself has the tongue on ye," admitted Rifleman McRory admiringly, "though I'm wonnering how'll you be schamin' to get another trench dug from the listening-post out to the Gineral."

"'Twill take some scheming," agreed another rifleman, "but maybe we can get round the officer that's in the listening-post to-night to let us drive a sap out."

"It's not him ye'll be getting round," said McRory, "for it's the Little Lad himself that's in it. But sure the Little Lad will be that glad to see me offer to take a pick in my hand that I believe he'd be willing to let me dig up his own grandfather's grave."

"We'll find some way when the time comes, never fear," said Sergeant Clancy, and the men willingly agreed to leave the matter in his capable hands.

Immediately after dark, the Little Lad, otherwise Lieute-nant Riley, led his party at a careful crawl and in wide-spaced single file out to the listening-post, while Brock and the Captain crawled out with a couple of men, a white tape, and a handful of pegs apiece to mark out the line of the new trenches converging from the outside ends of the curved main trench to the listening-post.

When they returned and reported their job complete, the working parties crawled cautiously out. There were plenty of flares being thrown up from the German lines and a more or less erratic rifle fire was crackling up and down the trenches on both sides, the Tearaways taking care to keep their bullets clear of the working party, to fire no more than enough to allay any German suspicions of a job being in hand, and not to provoke any extra hostility.

The working party crept out one by one, carrying their rifles and their trenching tools, dropping flat and still in the long grass every time a light flared, rising and crawling rapidly forward in the intervals of darkness. When at last they were strung out at distances of less than a man's length, they stealthily commenced operations. A line of filled sandbags was handed out from the main trench and passed along the chain of men until each had been provided with one.

Making the sand-bag a foundation for head cover, the men began cautiously to cut and scoop the soft ground and pile it up in front of them. The grass was long and rank, and in the shifting light the work went on unobserved for over an hour. The men, cramped and uncomfortable, with every muscle aching from head to foot, worked doggedly, knowing each five minutes' work, each handful of earth scooped out and thrown up, meant an extra point off the odds on a bullet reaching them when the Germans discovered their operations and opened fire on the working party.

They still worked only in the dark intervals between the flares, and, of course, in as deep a silence as they possibly could. Brock and the Captain crawled at intervals up and down the line with a word of praise or a reproach dropped here and there as it was needed. At the end of one trip, Brock crept into the listening-post and conversed in whispers with Riley, his fellow-conspirator.

"They're working like beavers," he said, "and, if the Boche doesn't twig the game for another half-hour, we'll have enough cover scooped out to go on without losing too many men from their fire."

Riley chuckled. "It's working fine," he said. "I'm only hoping that some ruffian doesn't spoil the game by crawling out and finding our General is no more than a false alarm."

"That would queer the pitch," agreed Brock, "but I don't fancy any one will try it. They all know the working party is liable to be discovered at any minute, and any one out in the open when that comes off, is going to be in a tight corner."

"There's a good many here," said Riley, "that would chance a few tight corners if they knew five thousand francs was at the other side of it; but I took the precaution to hint gently to Clancy that our machine gun was going to keep on spraying lead round the General all night, to discourage any private enterprise."

"Anyhow," said Brock, "I suppose the whole regiment's in it, and flatter themselves this trifle of digging is for the special benefit of their pockets. But what are those fellows of ours supposed to be digging at in the corner there!"

"That," whispered the Little Lad, grinning, "is merely an improving of the amenities of the listening-post and the beginning of a dugout shelter from bombs; at least, that's Clancy's suggestion, though I have a suspicion there will be no hurry to roof-in the dug-out and that its back-door will travel an unusual length out."

"Well, so long," said Brock; "I must sneak along again and have a look at the digging."

It was when he was half-way back to the main trench that it became apparent the German suspicions were aroused, and that something - a movement after a light flared, perhaps, or the line of a parapet beginning to show above the grass - had drawn their attention to the work.

Light after light commenced to toss in an unbroken stream from their parapet in the direction of the working party, and a score of bullets, obviously aimed at them, hissed close overhead.

"Glory be!" said Rifleman McRory, flattening himself to the ground. "It's a good foot and a half I have of head-cover, and I'm thinking it's soon we will be needing it, and all the rest we can get."

The flaring lights ceased again for a moment, and the men plied their tools in feverish haste to strengthen their scanty shelter against the storm they knew must soon fall upon them.

It came within a couple of minutes; again the lights streamed upward, and flares burst and floated down in dazzling balls of fierce white light, while the rifle-fire from the German parapet grew heavier and heavier. Concealment was no longer possible, and the word was passed to get along with the work in light or dark; and so, still lying flat upon their faces, and with the bullets hissing and whistling above them, slapping into the low parapet and into the bare ground beside them, the working party scooped and buried and scraped, knowing that every inch they could sink themselves or heighten their parapet added to their chance of life.

The work they had done gave them a certain amount of cover, at least for the vital parts of head and shoulders, but in the next half-hour there were many casualties, and man after man worked on with blood oozing through the hastily-applied bandage of a first field-dressing or crawled in under the scanty parapet and crouched there helplessly.

It was little use at that stage trying to bring in the wounded. To do so only meant exposing them to almost a certainty of another wound and of further casualties amongst the stretcher-bearers. One or two men were killed.

Lieutenant Riley, dragging himself along the line, found Rifleman McRory hard at work behind the shelter of a body rolled up on top of his parapet.

"It's killed he is," said McRory in answer to a question - "killed to the bone. He won't be feeling any more bullets that hit him, and it's himself would be the one to have said to use him this way."

Riley admitted the force of the argument and crept on. Work moved faster now that there was no need to wait for the periods between the lights; but the German fire also grew faster, and a machine gun began to pelt its bullets up and down the length of the growing parapet.

By now, fortunately, the separate chain of pits dug by each man were practically all connected up into a long, twisting, shallow trench. Down this trench the wounded were passed, and a fresh working party relieved the cramped and tired batch who had commenced the work.

In the main trench men had been hard at work filling sand-bags, and now these were passed out, dragged along from man to man, and piled up on the parapet, doubling the security of the workers and allowing them the greater freedom of rising to their knees to dig.

The rifles and maxims of the Tearaways had from the main trench kept up a steady volume of fire on the German parapet, in an endeavor to keep down its fire. They shot from the main trench in comparative safety, because the German fire was directed almost exclusively on the new trench.

Now that the new parapet had been heightened and

strengthened, the casualties behind it had almost ceased, and the Tearaways were quite reasonably flattering them-selves on the worst of the work being done and the worst of the dangers over. It appeared to them that the trench now provided quite sufficient shelter to fulfill both its ostensible object of allowing relief parties to move to and from the listening-post, and also their own private undertaking of attaining the dead General; but the O.C. and company commanders did not look on it in that light.

The order was to construct a firing trench, and that meant a good deal more work than had been done, so reliefs were kept going and the work progressed steadily all night, a good deal of impetus being given to it by some light German field-guns which commenced to scatter high-explosive shrapnel over the open ground.

The shooting, fortunately, was not very accurate, no doubt because, by the light of the flares, it was difficult for the German observers to direct their fire. But the hint was enough for the Tearaways, and they knew that daybreak would bring more accurate and more constant artillery fire upon the new position.

The British gunners had been warned not to open fire unless called upon, because a working party was in the open; but now the batteries were telephoned to with a request for shrapnel on the German parapets to keep down some of the heavy rifle fire.

Since the gunners had already registered the target of the German trench, their fire was just as accurate by night as it would be by day, and shell after shell burst over the German parapet, sweeping their trench with showers of shrapnel.

While all this was going on the men at the listening-post had tackled the job of driving their sap out to the German General. This work was done in a different fashion from the digging of the new trench.

The listening-post was merely a pit in the ground, originally a large shell crater, and deepened and widened until it was sufficiently large to hold half-a-dozen men. At one side of the pit the men commenced with pick and spade to hack out an opening like a very narrow doorway.

As the earth was broken down and shoveled back, the doorway gradually grew to be a passage. In this two men at a time worked in turn, the one on the right-hand side making a narrow cut that barely gave him shoulder-play, the second man on the left working a few paces in the rear and widening the passage.

Necessarily it was slow work, because only these two men could reach the face of the cut, and because it had to be of sufficient depth to allow a man to work upright without his head showing above the ground. But because they worked in short reliefs and put every ounce of energy into their task, they made surprising and unusual progress.

Lieutenant Riley, who was in command of the listening-post for that night, left the workers to themselves, both because it was necessary for him to keep a sharp look-out in order to give warning of any attempt to rush the working party, and because officially he was not supposed to know anything of any sap to an officially unrecognized dead German General.

When he was relieved after daybreak, Riley told the joke and explained the position to the subaltern who took over from him, and that subaltern in turn looked with a merely unofficial eye on the work of the sapping party. As the day and the work went on, it was quite obvious that a good many more men were working on the new trench than had been told off to it.

In the sap several fresh men were constantly awaiting their turn at the face with pick and shovel. The diggers did no more than five minutes' work, hacking and spading at top speed, yielding their tools to the next comer and retiring, panting and blowing and mopping their streaming brows.

A fairly constant fire was maintained by the artillery on both sides, the shells splashing and crashing on the open ground about the new trench and the German parapet. There was little wind, and as a result the smoke of the shell-bursts hung heavily and trailed slowly over the open space between the trenches, veiling to some extent the sapping operations and the new trench. On the latter a tendency was quickly displayed to slacken work and to treat the job as being sufficiently complete, but when it came to Lieutenant Riley's turn to take charge of a fresh relief of workers on the new trench, he very quickly succeeded in brisking up operations.

Arrived at the listening-post, he found Sergeant Clancy and spoke a few words to him.

"Clancy," he said gently, "the work along that new trench is going a great deal too slow."

"'Tis hard work, sorr," replied Clancy excusingly, "and you'll be remembering the boys have been at it all night."

"Quite so, Clancy," said Riley smoothly, "and since it has to be dug a good six foot deep, I am just thinking the best thing to do will be to take this other party off the sap and turn 'em along to help on the trench. I'm not denying, Clancy, that I've a notion what the sap is for, although I'm supposed to know nothing of it; but I don't care if the sap is made, and I do care that the trench is. Now do you think I had better stop them on the sap, or can the party in the trench put a bit more ginger into it?"

"I'll just step along the trench again, sorr," said Clancy anxiously, "and I don't think you'll be having need to grumble again."

He stepped along the trench, and he left an extraordinary increase of energy behind him as he went.

"And what use might it be to make it any deeper?" grumbled

McRory. "Sure it's deep enough for all we need it."

"May be," said Sergeant Clancy, with bitter sarcasm, "it's yourself that'll just be stepping up to the Colonel and saying friendly like to him: 'Prickles, me lad, it's deep enough we've dug to lave us get out to our German Gineral. 'Tisn't for you we're digging this trench,' you'll be saying, ''tis for our own pleasure entirely.' You might just let me know what the Colonel says to that."

"There's some talk," he said, a little further down the line, "of our being relieved from here to-morrow afternoon. I've told you what the Little Lad was saying about turning the sap party in to help here. It's pretty you'd look clearing out to-morrow and leaving another battalion to come in to take over your new trench and your new sap and your German Gineral and the gold in his britches pocket together." And with that parting shaft he moved on.

For the rest of that day and all that night work moved at speed, and when the O.C. made his tour of inspection the following morning he was as delighted as he was amazed at the work done - and that, as he told the Adjutant, was saying something. Up to now he had known nothing of the sap, merely expressing satisfaction - again mingled with amazement - when he saw the entrance to the sap, lightly roofed in with boards for a couple of yards and shut off beyond that by a curtain of sacking, and was told that the men were amusing themselves making a bomb-proof dug-out.

But on this last morning, when the sap had approached to within twenty or thirty feet of the white head which was its objective, the Colonel's attention was directed to the matter somewhat forcibly. He heard the roar of exploding heavy shells, and as the "*crump, crump,*" continued steadily, he telephoned from the headquarters dug-out in rear of the support line to ask the forward trenches what was happening.

While he waited an answer, a message came from the Brigade

saying that the artillery had reported heavy German shelling on a sap-head, and demanding to know what, where, and why was the sap-head referred to. While the Colonel was puzzling over this mysterious message and vainly trying to recall any sap-head within his sector of line, the regimental Padre came into the dug-out.

"I've just come from the dressing station," he said, "and there's a boy there, McRory, that has me fair bewildered with his ravings. He's wounded in the head with a shrapnel splinter, and, although he seems sane and sensible enough in other ways, he's been begging me and the doctor not to send him back to the hospital. Did ever ye hear the like, and him with a lump as big as the palm of my hand cut from his head to the bare bone, and bleeding like a stuck pig in an apoplexy?"

The Colonel looked at him vacantly, his mind between this and the other problem of the Brigade's message.

"And that's not all that's in it," went on the Padre. "The doctor was telling me that there's been a round dozen of the past two days' casualties begging that same thing - not to be sent away till we come out of the trenches. And to beat all, McRory, when he was told he was going just the minute the ambulance came, had a confab with the stretcher bearers, and I heard him arguing with them about 'his share,' and 'when they got the Gineral,' and 'my bit o' the fifty thousand francs.' It has me beat completely."

By now the Colonel was completely bewildered, and he began to wonder whether he or his battalion were hopelessly mad. It was extraordinary enough that the men should have dug so willingly and well, and without a grumble being heard or a complaint made.

It was still more extraordinary that more or less severely wounded men should not be ardently desirous of the safety and comfort and feeding of the hospitals; and on the top of all was this mysterious message of a sap apparently being made by his men voluntarily and without any sanction, much less the usual required pressure.

A message came from Captain Conroy, in the forward trench, to say that Riley was coming up to headquarters and would explain matters.

Riley and the explanation duly arrived. "Ould Prickles," inclined at first to be mightily wroth at the unauthorized digging of the sap, caught a twinkle in the Padre's eye; and a modest hint from the Little Lad reminding him of the speed and excellence of the new trenches, construction turned the scale. He burst into a roar of laughter, and the Padre joined him heartily, while the Little Lad stood beaming and chuckling complacently.

"I must tell the Brigadier this," gasped the O.C. at last. "He might have had a cross word or two to say about a sap being dug without orders, but, thank heaven, he's an Irishman, and a poorer joke would excuse a worse crime with him. But I'm wondering what's going to happen when they reach their General and find no francs, and no watch, and not even a General; and mind you, Riley, the sap must be stopped at once. I can't be having good men casualtied on an unofficial job. Will you see to that right away?"

The Little Lad's chuckling rose to open giggling.

"It's stopped now, sir," he said - "just before I came up here. And what's more, the General won't need explaining; the German gunners spied our sap, and, trying to drop a heavy shell on it - well, they dropped one on to the General. So now there isn't a General, only a hole in the ground where he was."

Ould Prickles' and the Padre's laughter bellowed again.

"I must tell that to the Brigadier, too," said the O.C.; "that finish to the joke will completely satisfy him."

"And I must go," said the Padre, rising, "and tell McRory, though I'm not just sure whether it will be after satisfying him quite so completely."

AT LAST

"WHEN WE BEGIN TO PUSH"

"Here we are," said the Colonel, halting his horse. "Fine view one gets from here."

"Rather a treat to be able to see over a bit of country again, after so many months of the flat," said, the Adjutant, reining up beside the other. They were halted on the top of a hill, or, father, the corner of an edge on a wide plateau. On two sides of them the ground fell away abruptly, the road they were on dipping sharply over the edge and sweeping round and downward in a well-graded slope along the face of the hill to the wide flats below. Over these flats they could see for many miles, miles of cultivated fields, of little woods, of gentle slopes. They could count the buildings of many farms, the roofs of half a dozen villages, the spires of twice as many churches, the tall chimneys and gaunt frame towers of scattered pit-heads. It had been raining all day, but now in the late afternoon the clouds had broken and the light of the low sun was tinging the landscape with a mellow golden glow.

"There's going to be a beautiful sunset presently," said the Colonel, "with all those heavy broken clouds about. Let's dismount and wait for a bit."

Both dismounted and handed their reins to the orderly, who, riding behind them, had halted when they did, but now at a sign came forward.

"We'll just stroll to that rise on the left," the Colonel said. "The best view should be from there."

The Adjutant lingered a moment. "Take their bits out, Trumpeter," he said, "and let them pick a mouthful of grass along the roadside."

A rough country track ran to the left off the main road, and the two walked along it a couple of hundred yards to where it plunged over the crest and ran steeply down the hillside. Another main road ran along the flat parallel with the hill foot, and along this crawled a long khaki column.

"Look at the light on those hills over there," said the Colonel. "Fine, isn't it?"

The Adjutant was busily engaged with the field-glasses he had taken from the case slung over his shoulder and was focusing them on the road below.

"I say," he remarked suddenly, "those are the Canadians. I didn't know the - th Division was so far south. Moving up front, too." The Colonel dropped his gaze to the road a moment and then swept it slowly over the country-side. "Yes," he said, "and this area is pretty well crowded with troops when you look closely."

The light on the distant hills was growing more golden and beautiful, the clouds were beginning to catch the first tints of the sunset, but neither men for the moment noticed these things, searching with their gaze the landscape below, sifting it over and picking out a battery of artillery camped in a big chalk-pit by the roadside, the slow-rising and drifting columns of blue smoke that curled up from a distant wood and told of the regiment encamped there, the long strings of horses converging on a big mine building for the afternoon watering, the lines of transport wagons parked on the outskirts of a village, the shifting khaki figures that stirred about every farm building in sight, the row of gray-painted motor-omnibuses, drawn up in a long line on a side road. The countryside that under a first look slept peacefully in the afternoon sunlight, that drowsed calmly in the easy quiet of an uneventful field and farm existence, proved under the closer searching look to be a teeming hive of activity, a close-packed camp of well-armed fighting men, a widespread net and chain of men and guns and horses. The peaceful countryside was overflowing with men and bristling with bayonets; every village was a crammed-full military cantonment, every barn stuffed with soldiers like an overfilled barracks.

The Adjutant whistled softly. "This," he said, and nodded again and again to the plain below, "this looks like business - at last."

"Yes," said the Colonel, "at last. It's going to be a very different story this time, when we begin to push things."

"Hark at the guns," said the Adjutant, and both stood silent a moment listening to the long, deep, rolling thunder that boomed steady and unbroken as surf on a distant beach. "And they're our guns too, mostly," went on the Adjutant. "I suppose we're firing more shells in an ordinary trench-war-routine day now than we dared fire in a month this time last year. Last year we were short of shells, the year before we were short of guns and shells and men. Now hear the guns and look down there at a few of the men."

Through the still air rose from below them the shrill crow of a farmyard rooster, the placid mooing of a cow, the calls and laughter of some romping children.

But the two on the hillside had no ear for these sounds of peace. They heard only that distant sullen boom of the rumbling guns, the throbbing foot-beats of the marching battalions below them, the plop-plopping hoofs and rattling wheels of wagons passing on their way up to the firing line with food for the guns.

"Our turn coming," said the Adjutant - "at last."

"Yes," the Colonel said, and repeated grimly - "at last."

Choose from Thousands of 1stWorldLibrary Classics By

Adolphus WilliamWard
Aesop
Agatha Christie
Alexander Aaronsohn
Alexander Kielland
Alexandre Dumas
Alfred Gatty
Alfred Ollivant
Alice Duer Miller
Alice Turner Curtis
Alice Dunbar
Ambrose Bierce
Amelia E. Barr
Andrew Lang
Andrew McFarland Davis
Anna Sewell
Annie Besant
Annie Hamilton Donnell
Annie Payson Call
Anton Chekhov
Arnold Bennett
Arthur Conan Doyle
Arthur Ransome
Atticus
B. M. Bower
Basil King
Bayard Taylor
Ben Macomber
Booth Tarkington
Bram Stoker
C. Collodi
C. E. Orr
C. M. Ingleby
Carolyn Wells
Catherine Parr Traill
Charles A. Eastman
Charles Dickens
Charles Dudley Warner
Charles Farrar Browne
Charles Ives
Charles Kingsley
Charles Lathrop Pack
Charles Whibley
Charles Willing Beale
Charlotte M. Braeme
Charlotte M.Yonge
Clair W. Hayes
Clarence Day Jr.
Clarence E. Mulford

Clemence Housman
Confucius
Cornelis DeWitt Wilcox
Cyril Burleigh
D. H. Lawrence
Daniel Defoe
David Garnett
Don Carlos Janes
Donald Keyhole
Dorothy Kilner
Dougan Clark
E. Nesbit
E.P.Roe
E. Phillips Oppenheim
Edgar Allan Poe
Edgar Rice Burroughs
Edith Wharton
Edward J. O'Biren
John Cournos
Edwin L. Arnold
Eleanor Atkins
Elizabeth Cleghorn
Gaskell
Elizabeth Von Arnim
Ellem Key
Emily Dickinson
Erasmus W. Jones
Ernie Howard Pie
Ethel Turner
Ethel Watts Mumford
Eugenie Foa
Eugene Wood
Evelyn Everett-Green
Everard Cotes
F. J. Cross
Federick Austin Ogg
Ferdinand Ossendowski
Francis Bacon
Francis Darwin
Frances Hodgson Burnett
Frank Gee Patchin
Frank Harris
Frank Jewett Mather
Frank L. Packard
Frederick Trevor Hill
Frederick Winslow Taylor
Friedrich Kerst
Friedrich Nietzsche
Fyodor Dostoyevsky

Gabrielle E. Jackson
Garrett P. Serviss
Gaston Leroux
George Ade
Geroge Bernard Shaw
George Ebers
George Eliot
George MacDonald
George Orwell
George Tucker
George W. Cable
George Wharton James
Gertrude Atherton
Grace E. King
Grant Allen
Guillermo A. Sherwell
Gulielma Zollinger
Gustav Flaubert
H. A. Cody
H. B. Irving
H. G. Wells
H. H. Munro
H. Irving Hancock
H. Rider Haggard
H. W. C. Davis
Hamilton Wright Mabie
Hans Christian Andersen
Harold Avery
Harold McGrath
Harriet Beecher Stowe
Harry Houidini
Helent Hunt Jackson
Helen Nicolay
Hendy David Thoreau
Henrik Ibsen
Henry Adams
Henry Ford
Henry Frost
Henry James
Henry Jones Ford
Henry Seton Merriman
Henry Wadsworth
Longfellow
Henry W Longfellow
Herbert A. Giles
Herbert N. Casson
Herman Hesse
Homer
Honore De Balzac

Horace Walpole
Horatio Alger, Jr.
Howard Pyle
Howard R. Garis
Hugh Lofting
Hugh Walpole
Humphry Ward
Ian Maclaren
Israel Abrahams
J.G.Austin
J. Henri Fabre
J. M. Barrie
J. Macdonald Oxley
J. S. Knowles
J. Storer Clouston
Jack London
Jacob Abbott
James Allen
James Lane Allen
James Andrews
James Baldwin
James DeMille
James Joyce
James Oliver Curwood
James Oppenheim
James Otis
Jane Austen
Jens Peter Jacobsen
Jerome K. Jerome
John Burroughs
John F. Kennedy
John Gay
John Glasworthy
John Habberton
John Joy Bell
John Milton
John Philip Sousa
Jonathan Swift
Joseph Carey
Joseph Conrad
Joseph Jacobs
Julian Hawthrone
Julies Vernes
Justin Huntly McCarthy
Kakuzo Okakura
Kenneth Grahame
Kate Langley Bosher
L. A. Abbot
L. T. Meade
L. Frank Baum
Laura Lee Hope

Laurence Housman
Leo Tolstoy
Leonid Andreyev
Lewis Carroll
Lilian Bell
Lloyd Osbourne
Louis Tracy
Louisa May Alcott
Lucy Fitch Perkins
Lucy Maud Montgomery
Lydia Miller Middleton
Lyndon Orr
M. H. Adams
Margaret E. Sangster
Margaret Vandercook
Maria Edgeworth
Maria Thompson Daviess
Mariano Azuela
Marion Polk Angellotti
Mark Overton
Mark Twain
Mary Austin
Mary Cole
Mary Rowlandson
Mary Wollstonecraft
Shelley
Max Beerbohm
Myra Kelly
Nathaniel Hawthrone
O. F. Walton
Oscar Wilde
Owen Johnson
P.G.Wodehouse
Paul and Mable Thorn
Paul G. Tomlinson
Paul Severing
Peter B. Kyne
Plato
R. Derby Holmes
R. L. Stevenson
Rabindranath Tagore
Rahul Alvares
Ralph Waldo Emmerson
Rene Descartes
Rex E. Beach
Richard Harding Davis
Richard Jefferies
Robert Barr
Robert Frost
Robert Gordon Anderson
Robert L. Drake

Robert Lansing
Robert Michael Ballantyne
Robert W. Chambers
Rosa Nouchette Carey
Ross Kay
Rudyard Kipling
Samuel B. Allison
Samuel Hopkins Adams
Sarah Bernhardt
Selma Lagerlof
Sherwood Anderson
Sigmund Freud
Standish O'Grady
Stanley Weyman
Stella Benson
Stephen Crane
Stewart Edward White
Stijn Streuvels
Swami Abhedananda
Swami Parmananda
T. S. Ackland
The Princess Der Ling
Thomas A. Janvier
Thomas A Kempis
Thomas Anderton
Thomas Bailey Aldrich
Thomas Bulfinch
Thomas De Quincey
Thomas H. Huxley
Thomas Hardy
Thomas More
Thornton W. Burgess
U. S. Grant
Valentine Williams
Victor Appleton
Virginia Woolf
Walter Scott
Washington Irving
Wilbur Lawton
Wilkie Collins
Willa Cather
Willard F. Baker
William Makepeace
Thackeray
William W. Walter
Winston Churchill
Yei Theodora Ozaki
Young E. Allison
Zane Grey